FUN 學美國英語 閱讀寫作 課本

AMERICAN SCHOOL TEXTBOOK

GRADE **4**
MP3 🔊

Reading & Writing

作者 Christine Dugan / Leslie Huber / Margot Kinberg / Miriam Meyers   譯者-林育珊

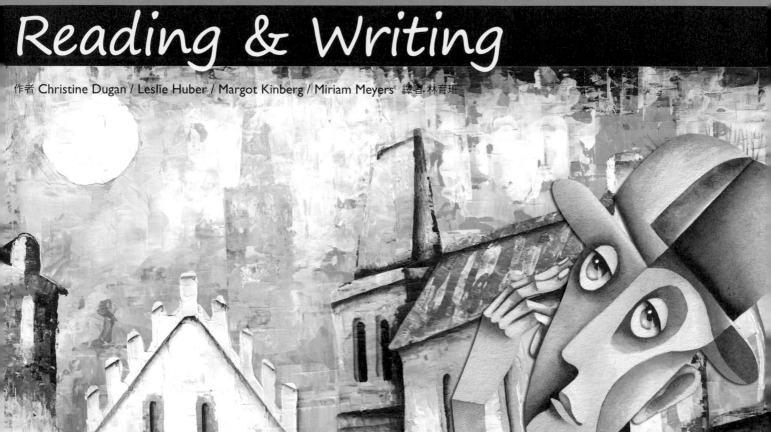

FUN 學美國英語 閱讀寫作 課本 4
American School Textbook: Reading & Writing

作　　者	Christine Dugan / Leslie Huber / Margot Kinberg / Miriam Meyers
譯　　者	林育珊
編　　輯	呂紹柔

封面設計	郭瀞暄
內文排版	田慧盈／郭瀞暄
製程管理	宋建文
出 版 者	寂天文化事業股份有限公司
電　　話	+886-(0)2-2365-9739
傳　　真	+886-(0)2-2365-9835
網　　址	www.icosmos.com.tw
讀者服務	onlineservice@icosmos.com.tw
出版日期	2013 年 9 月 初版一刷　(080101)

郵撥帳號　1998620-0　　寂天文化事業股份有限公司

· 劃撥金額 600（含）元以上者，郵資免費。

· 訂購金額 600 元以下者，加收 65 元運費。

【若有破損，請寄回更換，謝謝。】

HOW TO USE THIS BOOK

The **Skill Overview** provides background information about the skill focus for the lesson.

Reading Passage

The **Lesson Number** and **Reading Skill** are clearly identified.

The **Reading Tip** provides guidance for reading each lesson.

Critical Vocabulary words from the passage are listed.

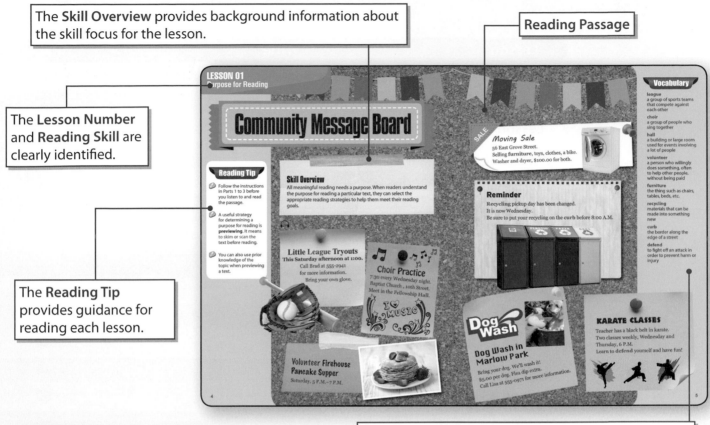

Power Up summarizes the key terminology and ideas for each lesson.

Comprehension Review helps determine your level of mastery of these strategies and skills.

Word Power reinforces the importance of the critical vocabularies with pictures.

The interactive **Reading Skill Comprehension Practice** helps reinforce the strategy being taught.

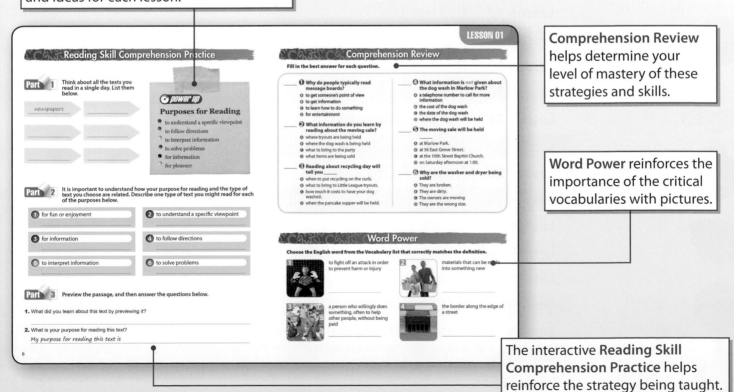

Contents Chart

Lesson	Title	Page
Lesson 1	Community Message Board	4
Lesson 2	Harriet Tubman	8
Lesson 3	Keep Your Eyes on the Prize	12
Lesson 4	The Bear and the Two Travelers	16
Lesson 5	Mohandas Gandhi, The Great Soul	20
Lesson 6	Honeycomb	24
Lesson 7	The Journey to Space	28
Lesson 8	Jumpin' Johnny	32
Lesson 9	Hydroponics	36
Lesson 10	Benjamin Franklin, The Death of a Great Man	40
Lesson 11	Interdependence of Life	44
Lesson 12	City Summer	48
Lesson 13	Alarm Clock	52
Lesson 14	American Indians in the 1800s	56
Lesson 15	Who Were Abolitionists?	60
Lesson 16	Architectural Shapes	64
Lesson 17	Bad Hair Day	68
Lesson 18	Biomes	72
Lesson 19	Marc van Roosmalen: Fighter for Biodiversity	76
Lesson 20	Velociraptor	80
Lesson 21	The Bundle of Sticks	84
Lesson 22	A New Grandfather	88
Lesson 23	Nom de Plume Research	92
Lesson 24	Author Envy	96
Lesson 25	Upside Down	100
Lesson 26	City of the Aztecs	104
Lesson 27	Chapter 2: Diseases, Germs All Around Us	108
Lesson 28	Ancient China	112
Lesson 29	If an Atom in My Lunchroom Could Talk	116
Lesson 30	The Test	120
Review Test		124

Reading Skill	Subject
Purpose for Reading	Language and Literature
Previewing	Social Studies ★ History and Geography
Cause and Effect—Plot	Language and Literature
Making Inferences	Language and Literature
Main Idea and Details	Social Studies ★ History and Geography
Titles and Headings to Predict	Science
Selecting Reading Material	Science
Character Development	Language and Literature
Logical Order	Science
Headings to Determine Main Ideas	Social Studies ★ History and Geography
Topic Sentences to Predict	Science
Literary Devices	Language and Literature
Sequential Order	Language and Literature
Paraphrasing	Social Studies ★ History and Geography
Summary Sentences	Social Studies ★ History and Geography
Reflecting on What Has Been Learned	Language and Literature
Use of Language	Language and Literature
Compare and Contrast	Science
Adjust and Extend Knowledge	Science
Topic Sentences to Determine Main Ideas	Science
Author's Devices	Language and Literature
Author's Point of View	Language and Literature
Drawing Conclusions	Language and Literature
Proposition and Support	Language and Literature
Graphic Features	Science
Mental Images	Social Studies ★ History and Geography
Chapter Titles to Determine Main Ideas	Science
Chronological Order	Social Studies ★ History and Geography
Fact and Opinion	Language and Literature
Questioning	Language and Literature

Community Message Board

Reading Tip

- Follow the instructions in Parts 1 to 3 before you listen to and read the passage.

- A useful strategy for determining a purpose for reading is **previewing**. It means to skim or scan the text before reading.

- You can also **use prior knowledge** of the topic when previewing a text.

Skill Overview

All meaningful reading needs a purpose. When readers understand the purpose for reading a particular text, they can select the appropriate reading strategies to help them meet their reading goals.

Little League Tryouts
This Saturday afternoon at 1:00.
Call Brad at 555-2941
for more information.
Bring your own glove.

Choir Practice
7:30 every Wednesday night.
Baptist Church, 10th Street.
Meet in the Fellowship Hall.

Volunteer Firehouse
Pancake Supper
Saturday, 5 P.M.–7 P.M.

4

Moving Sale

56 East Grove Street.
Selling **furniture**, toys, clothes, a bike.
Washer and dryer, $100.00 for both.

Reminder

Recycling pickup day has been changed.
It is now Wednesday.
Be sure to put your recycling on the **curb** before 8:00 A.M.

Dog Wash in Marlow Park

Bring your dog. We'll wash it!
$5.00 per dog. Flea dip extra.
Call Lisa at 555-0971 for more information.

KARATE CLASSES

Teacher has a black belt in karate.
Two classes weekly,
Wednesday and Thursday, 6 P.M.
Learn to **defend** yourself and have fun!

Reading Skill Comprehension Practice

Part 1 Think about all the texts you read in a single day. List them below.

> newspapers

Part 2 It is important to understand how your purpose for reading and the type of text you choose are related. Describe one type of text you might read for each of the purposes below.

1 for fun or enjoyment

2 to understand a specific viewpoint

3 for information

4 to follow directions

5 to interpret information

6 to solve problems

Part 3 Preview the passage, and then answer the questions below.

1. What did you learn about this text by previewing it?

2. What is your purpose for reading this text?

My purpose for reading this text is

Comprehension Review

Fill in the best answer for each question.

_____ ❶ **Why do people typically read message boards?**
- Ⓐ to get someone's point of view
- Ⓑ to get information
- Ⓒ to learn how to do something
- Ⓓ for entertainment

_____ ❷ **What information do you learn by reading about the moving sale?**
- Ⓐ where tryouts are being held
- Ⓑ where the dog wash is being held
- Ⓒ what to bring to the party
- Ⓓ what items are being sold

_____ ❸ **Reading about recycling day will tell you _____**
- Ⓐ when to put recycling on the curb.
- Ⓑ what to bring to Little League tryouts.
- Ⓒ how much it costs to have your dog washed.
- Ⓓ when the pancake supper will be held.

_____ ❹ **What information is _not_ given about the dog wash in Marlow Park?**
- Ⓐ a telephone number to call for more information
- Ⓑ the cost of the dog wash
- Ⓒ the date of the dog wash
- Ⓓ where the dog wash will be held

_____ ❺ **The moving sale will be held _____**
- Ⓐ at Marlow Park.
- Ⓑ at 56 East Grove Street.
- Ⓒ at the 10th Street Baptist Church.
- Ⓓ on Saturday afternoon at 1:00.

_____ ❻ **Why are the washer and dryer being sold?**
- Ⓐ They are broken.
- Ⓑ They are dirty.
- Ⓒ The owners are moving.
- Ⓓ They are the wrong size.

Word Power

Choose the English word from the Vocabulary list that correctly matches the definition.

 to fight off an attack in order to prevent harm or injury

_____

 materials that can be made into something new

_____

 a person who willingly does something, often to help other people, without being paid

_____

 the border along the edge of a street

_____

Harriet Tubman

Skill Overview

Previewing helps readers get a sense of what is to come in a text and connect it to their background knowledge. When readers are able to anticipate topics and understand how information is organized in a text, they can choose appropriate strategies for reading the material.

🎧 02

When Harriet Tubman was born, around the year 1820, she was named Araminta Ross. Her nickname was Minty. When she grew up, Minty went by the name of Harriet, which was her mother's name. Her father was called Old Ben.

Harriet grew up on a **plantation** on the eastern shore of Maryland. Harriet and her parents were **slaves** on the plantation. Harriet was a slave because her parents were slaves. She had many brothers and sisters, some of whom worked for other farmers.

When Harriet was young, she played with the other children during the day. An elderly woman watched all the children while their parents worked in the fields.

At night, Harriet slept on the dirt floor of her family's cabin. Sometimes she listened to the adults talk about **freedom**. Although she did not know what freedom was, she thought

Vocabulary

plantation
an agricultural estate worked by laborers

slave
a person who is legally owned by someone else and has to work for them

freedom
the condition or right of being able or allowed to do, say, think, etc., whatever you want

escape
to get free from something or someone

convince
to persuade someone

⚙**free state**
a state in the United States in which slavery was not legal in the mid-1800s

desire
to want something

conductor
an organizer of the network of people secretly helping slaves escape to freedom, called the *Underground Railroad*

it sounded wonderful and wanted to learn more about it. At the age of seven, Harriet tried to **escape** from the plantation, but she did not succeed.

Harriet was curious when she heard the word *freedom*. When she was old enough to understand what it meant, she wanted it, too. Harriet tried to talk about freedom to her mother, but her mother was afraid to hear about it. However, Harriet's father was always willing to talk of freedom. Old Ben wanted to prepare his daughter to be free.

Harriet married John Tubman, a free man, in 1844. This made Harriet want freedom even more. John did not want Harriet to try to escape, but Harriet's father disagreed with John. Old Ben taught Harriet about living in the woods because he believed that she needed to know how to survive. He showed her how to follow the North Star and taught her how to swim and start a fire. She learned how to catch and skin animals to eat.

Harriet planned to run away several times, but she always turned back because the time was not right. In 1849, she found out that she might be sold. This **convinced** her that it was time to escape.

Many people helped Harriet along the way. After days of running and hiding, she finally made it to the **free state** of Pennsylvania. Harriet found a job in Philadelphia, Pennsylvania. She worked hard and saved her money. With a **desire** to help other slaves, she became the first female **conductor** on the Underground Railroad.

Reading Skill Comprehension Practice

One way to **skim** the passage is to <u>quickly read the first sentence of each paragraph</u> to see where the story is headed.

 **Preview the passage. Then answer the questions below.**

YES	NO	
☐	☐	Does the text include any **pictures** that give you information about the topic?
☐	☐	Is the text **written in paragraphs**? Explain what this tells you.
☐	☐	Are there any **headings**, **titles**, or other text features in the passage?

What does this **text format** tell you about the topic?

_____

 **Skim the passage about Harriet Tubman. Record two ideas about the text below.**

1. Harriet was curious when she heard the word freedom.

2. _____

3. _____

 **Use picture clues to help you preview the passage. What ideas do you have about the passage after looking at the pictures? Write them below.**

Comprehension Review

Fill in the best answer for each question.

_____ ❶ The title tells you that this passage is *mostly* about _____
- Ⓐ Old Ben.
- Ⓑ Harriet Tubman.
- Ⓒ Pennsylvania.
- Ⓓ Maryland.

_____ ❷ What is an important word in this passage?
- Ⓐ freedom
- Ⓑ plantation
- Ⓒ animals
- Ⓓ children

_____ ❸ What kind of text is this passage?
- Ⓐ a list of instructions
- Ⓑ an experiment
- Ⓒ the story of someone's life
- Ⓓ the history of Pennsylvania

_____ ❹ When did Harriet Tubman escape from slavery?
- Ⓐ when she was born
- Ⓑ when she married John Tubman
- Ⓒ after she found out she might be sold
- Ⓓ while her parents worked in the fields

_____ ❺ What is one thing Old Ben did *not* teach Harriet to do?
- Ⓐ read
- Ⓑ skin animals
- Ⓒ build a fire
- Ⓓ follow the North Star

_____ ❻ Why was Harriet Tubman called a *conductor*?
- Ⓐ She worked on a real train.
- Ⓑ She led an orchestra.
- Ⓒ She was a slave on a Southern plantation.
- Ⓓ She led people, just as a train conductor does.

Word Power

Choose the English word from the Vocabulary list that correctly matches the definition.

1. a state in the United States in which slavery was not legal in the mid-1800s

_____

2. an organizer of the network of people secretly helping slaves escape to freedom, called the *Underground Railroad*

_____

3. to want something

_____

4. an agricultural estate worked by laborers

_____

Skill Overview

Cause and effect is a pattern in text that explains the result of an event or occurrence and the reasons it happened. When readers recognize a cause-and-effect structure in a text, they can use appropriate strategies to better understand the material.

Reading Tip

Follow the instruction in Part 1 before you listen to and read the passage.

Keep Your Eyes on the Prize

When I was 14, my father bought me a great old **vintage** car. Even though the body was still in relatively good shape, everything else needed work. My father reminded me that Grandpa Bill enjoyed tinkering with vintage cars. If I asked him nicely, he would probably help me fix up the old **junker**. "You have two years to work on her before you get your driver's **license**," my father reminded me, "and that should give you plenty of time to get her running. You'll have to use your own money for parts, though, because I've done all I can do just shelling out the cash to buy her."

As you can imagine, I was excited to be 14 and already have my own car. And not just any car—a convertible. What could be cooler? Also, I **appreciated** the fact that the car and I were born the same year. Well, all right, cars aren't born...they're made, but you know what I mean.

When Grandpa arrived the next day, he stood back and gave old "Blue," the name I had given the car, a long **assessment**. "She looks **adequate** on the outside," he said at last, "but it's what's on the interior that counts. Let's lift her up and check her out. You get something to write on, and I'll tell you what you're going to need."

I hurriedly collected my notebook and pencil and returned to find Grandpa already putting her up on blocks. "Some of the **repairing** we can do ourselves, which means all it will cost you is parts. Anything major will have to be done at Eddy's Garage. It certainly isn't going to be cheap, you know." He stepped back for a moment and put his arm around my shoulder. "Whatever the cost or hard work, remember to keep your eyes on the prize. Imagine yourself **cruising** in the driver's seat of your car. And before you know it...there you'll be."

Vocabulary

✪vintage
old but still having interest and quality

✪junker
a car that needs many repairs

license
an official document that gives you permission to drive

appreciate
to recognize and value how good someone or something is

assessment
the act of judging or deciding the amount, value, or quality of something

adequate
enough, or satisfactory, for a particular purpose

repairing
the act of fixing something that is broken or damaged

cruise
to drive around for enjoyment

Reading Skill Comprehension Practice

 **Part 1** Read each cause below. Then write a possible effect.

CAUSE	EFFECT
1. A dog ran out into the street in front of a moving car.	1. _____
2. I broke my mom's rule and had a cookie before dinner.	2. _____
3. I decided to watch TV rather than study for my math test.	3. _____

Part 2 Find an example of cause and effect in the passage. Write it in the boxes below.

CAUSE His father bought him an old vintage car.

EFFECT He needs to save money to repair his car.

Part 3 List the words or phrases in the passage that indicate it has a cause-and-effect pattern.

If I

Comprehension Review

Fill in the best answer for each question.

_____ **① Why does the narrator have to use his own money for parts for the car?**

Ⓐ His grandfather enjoys tinkering with vintage cars.

Ⓑ The body is in good shape.

Ⓒ His father did all he could just to buy the car.

Ⓓ The car is a vintage automobile.

_____ **② Why will some of the repairs be cheaper than others?**

Ⓐ They will be done at Eddy's Garage.

Ⓑ The narrator and his grandpa will do the work themselves.

Ⓒ The narrator is a mechanic.

Ⓓ The car and the narrator were born in the same year.

_____ **③ What will be the effect of all the hard work and expenses?**

Ⓐ a trip to Eddy's garage

Ⓑ an old junker

Ⓒ a list of parts

Ⓓ the chance to cruise in the driver's seat

_____ **④ "You'll have to use your own money for parts, though, because I've done all I can do just shelling out the cash to buy her."**

What does _shelling out_ mean in this sentence?

Ⓐ spending

Ⓑ seashells

Ⓒ tinkering

Ⓓ shellfish

_____ **⑤ What is another term for _tinkering_?**

Ⓐ singing

Ⓑ fiddling with

Ⓒ building

Ⓓ driving

_____ **⑥ Why did the narrator ask Grandpa Bill for help?**

Ⓐ The narrator paid for parts for the car.

Ⓑ Some of the repairs had to be done at Eddy's Garage.

Ⓒ Grandpa Bill likes tinkering with vintage cars.

Ⓓ The car is the same age as Grandpa Bill.

Word Power

Choose the English word from the Vocabulary list that correctly matches the definition.

 to drive around for enjoyment

_____

 a car that needs many repairs

_____

 old but still having interest and quality

_____

 the act of fixing something that is broken or damaged

_____

Reading Tip

An author does not always include every bit of information necessary to tell a story because it might make the story too wordy or boring. Sometimes, you must "read between the lines."

One way to make inferences is by relating a story or character to your personal experience or knowledge.

The Bear and the Two Travelers

Skill Overview

Making an inference is the process of **judging**, **concluding**, or **reasoning** based on given information. As readers learn to interpret text and "read between the lines," they will learn to get to the intended message. Readers can also use inference to discover the meaning of unclear words, terms, or concepts.

This is a **fable** of two men who were traveling together, walking through the woods on their way to a final destination. Suddenly, a bear **appeared** before them on their path and **frightened** them.

Man 1: "I didn't think twice, but climbed quickly into a tree to save myself by hiding in the branches."

Man 2: "I followed my fellow traveler but **tripped**. Knowing that I would soon be **attacked**, I remained on the ground, motionless."

Vocabulary

fable
a short story that tells a general truth

appear
to start to be seen or be present

frighten
to make someone feel fear

✪**trip**
to lose your balance after knocking your foot against something when you are walking or running

attack
to try to hurt or defeat someone using violence

✪**nuzzle**
to push or rub with one's nose

descend
to climb down

misfortune
an unfortunate event or disaster

Man 1: "From my safe spot, I watched the bear as he felt the man lying on the ground, smelling him and **nuzzling** him all over with his snout."

Man 2: "I held my breath and pretended to be dead."

The bear soon left, for it is said a bear will not touch a dead body. When the bear was definitely gone, the other traveler **descended** from the tree and jokingly asked his friend a question.

Man 1: "What was it the bear whispered in your ear?"

Man 2: "He gave me this advice: Never travel with a friend who deserts you at the approach of danger."

The moral of this fable is "**Misfortune** tests the sincerity of friends."

Reading Skill Comprehension Practice

 **1** Think about a personal experience that this passage reminds you of. Record your ideas below.

Text-to-self Connection

My text-to-self connection is that _____

 **2** Make inferences about the passage to answer the questions below.

1. Why did the first man climb the tree without helping his friend?

_____

2. How did the second man feel about being left in danger?

_____

3. How did the second man likely feel about his friend making a joke once they were out of danger?

_____

4. How might this experience have changed the friendship between the two men?

_____

 **3** Think about another text this passage reminds you of. Record your ideas below.

Text-to-text Connection

This passage reminds me of _____

Comprehension Review

Fill in the best answer for each question.

_____ ❶ **What inference can you make about the man in the tree?**

Ⓐ He wants to protect his friend.

Ⓑ He likes bears.

Ⓒ He is a very brave person.

Ⓓ He knows bears can be dangerous.

_____ ❷ **The man on the ground _____**

Ⓐ has probably heard that bears will not touch a dead body.

Ⓑ is probably not afraid of bears.

Ⓒ is probably asleep.

Ⓓ probably knows nothing about bears.

_____ ❸ *When the bear was definitely gone, the other traveler descended from the tree and jokingly asked his friend a question.*

What can we infer about the traveler in the tree based on this sentence from the passage?

Ⓐ He thought his friend was hurt.

Ⓑ He thought the bear was still there.

Ⓒ He did not think his friend was in danger.

Ⓓ He was looking for the bear.

_____ ❹ *This is a fable of two men who were traveling together, walking through the woods on their way to a final destination.*

Because this is a fable, what can we infer?

Ⓐ The bear will come back and catch the men.

Ⓑ The story has a moral, or lesson.

Ⓒ The two men will remain friends.

Ⓓ The two men will reach their destination.

_____ ❺ *"I didn't think twice."*

What does this expression mean?

Ⓐ I acted right away.

Ⓑ I didn't know what was going on.

Ⓒ I thought for a long time.

Ⓓ I thought many times.

_____ ❻ **Why did the second traveler *not* climb the tree to safety?**

Ⓐ He thought he would be safer on the ground.

Ⓑ He did not see the bear.

Ⓒ He tripped and fell.

Ⓓ He knew there was no bear.

Word Power

Choose the English word from the Vocabulary list that correctly matches the definition.

 **1** to push or rub with one's nose

_____

 **2** to climb down

_____

 **3** an unfortunate event or disaster

_____

 **4** to try to hurt or defeat someone using violence

_____

Reading Tip

Nonfiction passages always have a main, or central, idea that is the most important thing about the text.

MOHANDAS GANDHI, THE GREAT SOUL

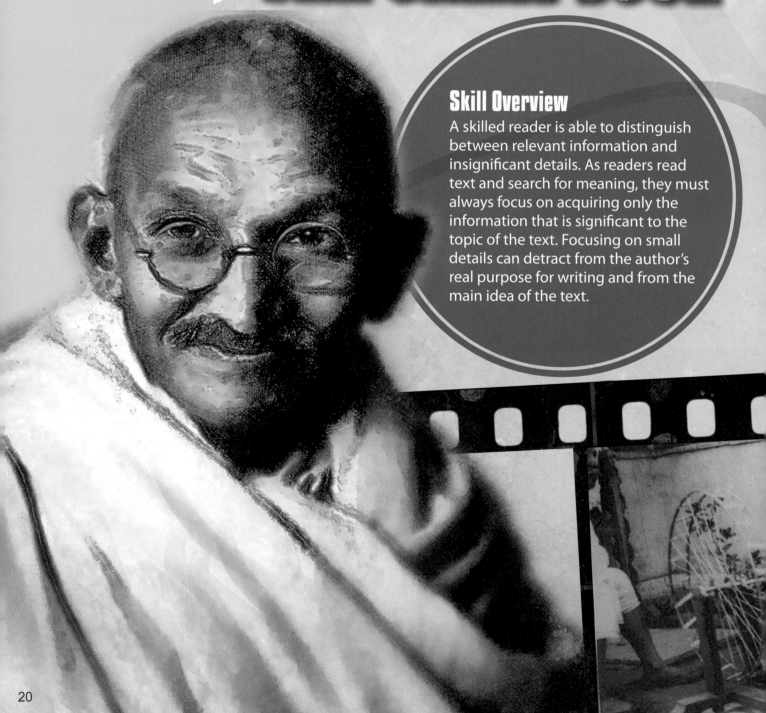

Skill Overview

A skilled reader is able to distinguish between relevant information and insignificant details. As readers read text and search for meaning, they must always focus on acquiring only the information that is significant to the topic of the text. Focusing on small details can detract from the author's real purpose for writing and from the main idea of the text.

🎧 05

In 1915, Mohandas Gandhi and his family returned to India. Gandhi started building centers for people to learn his way of life. He wanted people to **serve** their **communities**. He also won **support** for satyagraha. *Satyagraha* is a **philosophy**, or way of thinking. It was developed by Gandhi.

The people of India were still under British rule. Many of the British laws were unfair to the Indians. Gandhi taught the people satyagraha to change what was unfair. He worked on one **cause** after another. In 1919, new laws took away more freedoms across all of India. Mohandas Gandhi—now called Mahatma—began to work against the laws. He **captured** the attention of everyone in India and much of the world. Now, the people of India were working for their country's independence.

There were many important events during Gandhi's years in India. One such event was the Salt March of 1930. Britain charged the Indians a tax on salt. Also, only the British were allowed to make the salt. So Gandhi led a large group of people on a march. They marched 165 miles to the Arabian Sea. There, they made salt by evaporating seawater.

Gandhi was often jailed and **threatened**, but he continued his work. In 1947, he **proved** how powerful satyagraha was. After 200 years of British rule, India became a free country.

Gandhi during the Salt March, March 1930

Reading Skill Comprehension Practice

 **Part 1** Write one important fact and one insignificant fact about Gandhi below.

Important Fact

1. Gandhi worked for many years to help India become a free country.

2. _____

Insignificant Fact

1. Gandhi returned to India in 1915.

2. _____

Part 2 Imagine that you are telling a stranger about yourself. Write three important facts below.

1. _____

2. _____

3. _____

Part 3 Read the two sentences beside each topic below.
Decide which sentence is relevant, and mark it with an "R."
Decide which sentence is irrelevant, and mark it with an "I."

1 Olympic Games

_____ The Olympic Games invite the finest athletes from around the world to participate.

_____ Ice skaters often fall in the middle of their routines.

2 Communicating with Technology

_____ It is essential that you save your work while working on the computer.

_____ Technology has changed the way that people around the globe talk to each other.

3 School Uniforms

_____ Schools often require students to wear uniforms so that they are not distracted from their studies.

_____ On rainy days, most students wear raincoats and boots to stay dry.

Comprehension Review

Fill in the best answer for each question.

_____ ❶ **The Salt March of 1930 was a protest against_____**
- Ⓐ Mahatma Gandhi.
- Ⓑ unfair British laws and taxes.
- Ⓒ the people of India.
- Ⓓ satyagraha.

_____ ❷ **How long was India under British rule?**
- Ⓐ one years
- Ⓑ 10 years
- Ⓒ 200 year
- Ⓓ 750 years

_____ ❸ **At the Arabian Sea, the people of India made salt by _____**
- Ⓐ buying it from other countries.
- Ⓑ taking over British salt factories.
- Ⓒ evaporating seawater.
- Ⓓ boiling river water.

_____ ❹ **What was another name given to Mohandas Gandhi?**
- Ⓐ Mahatma
- Ⓑ India
- Ⓒ satyagraha
- Ⓓ Arabian Sea

_____ ❺ **Which is probably a reason that Mohandas Gandhi was often jailed and threatened?**
- Ⓐ He supported British rule in India.
- Ⓑ India became a free country in 1947.
- Ⓒ He was British.
- Ⓓ He supported Indian independence.

_____ ❻ **What was the purpose of satyagraha?**
- Ⓐ to change what was unfair
- Ⓑ to return India to British rule
- Ⓒ to bring Mohandas Gandhi to power
- Ⓓ the Salt March of 1930

Word Power

Choose the English word from the Vocabulary list that correctly matches the definition.

 something that deserves support

_____

 to catch or attract

_____

 to be harassed or treated poorly

_____

 approval or acceptance of someone or something

_____

Reading Tip

 Follow the instruction in Part 1 before you listen to and read the passage.

Skill Overview

Meaning clues such as titles and headings help readers increase their comprehension. By looking closely at titles and headings, readers can find clues about the main ideas of the text. These clues can help readers make meaningful predictions.

HONEYCOMB

06

Honeybees live in hives, which can often be found in **hollow** trees. A hive **contains** honeycomb. The honeycomb is made of many three-dimensional shapes called *cells*. The bees store honey and larvae in the cells.

Each honeycomb cell is a hexagonal prism. This hexagonal prism gets its name from the shape of its bases. Its bases are hexagons. These are two-dimensional shapes with six sides. Honeycomb hexagons form a pattern of shapes. These shapes fit together with no gaps or overlaps.

Patterns like this one are called *tessellations*. A tessellation is created when a shape is **repeated** over and over again, covering a plane without any gaps or **overlaps**. The word *tessellate* means to form or arrange small pieces in a checkered or mosaic pattern. The word *tessellate* is from the Greek word *tesseres*, which means "four." A regular polygon has three, four, five, or more sides and angles that are all **equal**. A **regular** tessellation is made up of **congruent** regular polygons. *Regular* means that the sides of the polygon are all the same length. *Congruent* means that the polygons that you put together are all the same size and shape.

PERFECT TESSELLATIONS

Only three shapes make perfect tessellations on their own. They are squares, equilateral triangles, and regular hexagons.

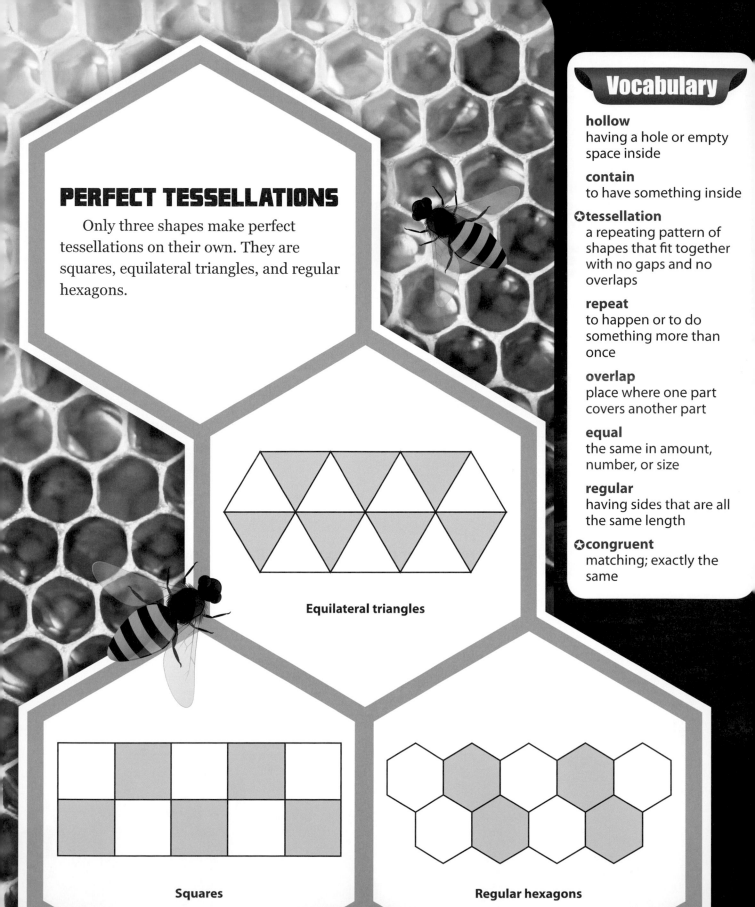

Equilateral triangles

Squares

Regular hexagons

Part 1 Think about what the title and heading tell you about the passage. Write your predictions below.

HONEYCOMB
PERFECT TESSELLATIONS

_____

_____

_____

_____

power up

One reading skill is to **make predictions** about a passage before reading.

To use this skill most effectively, you should continue to **make and revise your predictions as you read.**

Doing this keeps you motivated and focused on your reading because you are always reading ahead to see if your predictions are correct.

Part 2 Reread your predictions from Part 1. How do these predictions compare with the content of the passage? Write your ideas below.

_____

_____

_____

_____

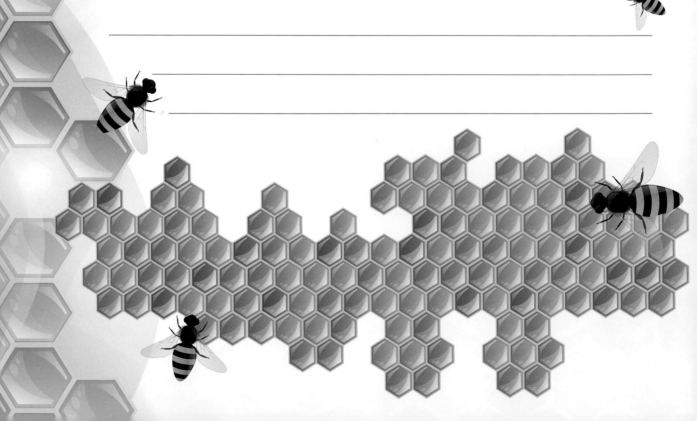

Comprehension Review

Fill in the best answer for each question.

_____ **❶ The title "Honeycomb" is a clue that this passage is about a _____**
- Ⓐ what bears eat.
- Ⓑ hair products.
- Ⓒ beehives.
- Ⓓ prisms.

_____ **❷ Based on the heading "Perfect Tessellations," what pattern is likely used in honeycombs?**
- Ⓐ a hive
- Ⓑ a perfect tessellation
- Ⓒ a regular hexagon
- Ⓓ a larva

_____ **❸ The title and heading tell you that you are probably going to read about _____**
- Ⓐ honeycomb tessellations.
- Ⓑ how bees make honeycombs.
- Ⓒ what bees use honeycombs for.
- Ⓓ where most honeycombs are found.

_____ **❹ _A regular polygon has three, four, or five, or more sides and angles that are all equal._**
   What does _regular_ mean in this sentence?
- Ⓐ medium sides
- Ⓑ very large sides
- Ⓒ very small sides
- Ⓓ sides of equal length

_____ **❺ What is a pattern that repeats itself with no gaps or overlaps called?**
- Ⓐ a tessellation
- Ⓑ a plane
- Ⓒ a prism
- Ⓓ a polygon

_____ **❻ Which shape does _not_ make a perfect tessellation on its own?**
- Ⓐ a square
- Ⓑ a circle
- Ⓒ a regular hexagon
- Ⓓ an equilateral triangle

Word Power

Choose the English word from the Vocabulary list that correctly matches the definition.

1 matching; exactly the same

_____

2 place where one part covers another part

_____

3 a repeating pattern of shapes that fit together with no gaps and no overlaps

_____

4 to happen or to do something more than once

_____

THE JOURNEY TO SPACE

Reading Tip

- Follow the instruction in Part 1 before you listen to and read the passage.

- You will read a passage about space exploration. Are you interested in reading a passage with this title?

Skill Overview

Readers' selection of reading material helps set a purpose for reading. When readers have a purpose for reading, they can focus on the content and better understand the text. Readers should consider many factors when selecting reading material, including **recommendations of others**, **personal interests**, **knowledge of authors**, and **text difficulty**.

07

The space race began in 1957 when the Soviet Union **launched** Sputnik 1. This was the world's first manmade **satellite**. Four years later, Soviet **cosmonaut** Yuri Gagarin became the first person to **pilot** a spacecraft in outer space.

Today, the largest space research group is in the United States. It is the National Aeronautics and Space Administration (NASA). Its Apollo 11 **mission** made the United States the first country to put a person on the Moon. In 1969, astronaut Neil Armstrong became the first person to walk on the Moon. The first words he spoke there are famous. He said, "One small step for man, one giant **leap** for mankind."

Apollo 11 crew

Apollo 11

Pioneer 10

NASA later developed the space shuttle, which is a spacecraft that can be used over and over. Since 1981, the space shuttle **fleet** has made more than 100 flights. Sadly, two crews were lost in tragic accidents.

In 1983, the space probe Pioneer 10 became the first manmade object to leave the solar system. It was launched 11 years earlier!

OUR BASE IN SPACE

Did you know there is a laboratory floating in outer space? It is called the International Space Station, or ISS. It is one of the brightest objects in the night sky. It is like a home in space: Astronauts live there and carry out experiments. People from 16 nations have worked on it. There are always at least two people on board. The first crew got there in 2000. Most crew members stay about six months.

THE FUTURE OF SPACE

What does the future hold for space **exploration**? NASA's plans for the future will take us to new heights! The next manned trip to the Moon is planned for 2018. This mission will possibly last about seven days. Scientists want astronauts to be able to produce water, fuel, and other necessities for life. Can homes on the Moon be far behind? There are also plans for astronauts to visit Mars by 2028. This would be a much longer mission. Astronauts could be on the planet's surface for 500 days!

Pluto should get a visit from Earth, too. Pluto is a dwarf planet at the edge of the solar system. In January 2006, NASA launched the New Horizons spacecraft. It began a very long trip and is due to reach Pluto in 2015. The unmanned spacecraft will fly by Pluto and send images and data back to Earth. New Horizons is sure to find surprises that will help us learn more about our solar system and our universe.

Sputnik 1

Yuri Gagarin

The International Space Station

New Horizons lifts off for more space exploration

Reading Skill Comprehension Practice

Part 1 Decide whether a story about space exploration is the kind of text you would choose to read. Explain why or why not.

Part 2 Answer the questions below about what kinds of books you would choose to read.

1. What is your favorite book? Why?

   My favorite book is A Dog's Purpose because it's very touching and inspiring.

2. Who is your favorite author? Why?

   My favorite author is Nicholas Sparks because I enjoy reading his love stories.

3. Have you ever recommended a book to someone else? If so, what book was it, and why did you recommend it?

   Yes, I did recommend the books in A Song of Ice and Fire series to my friends because they are fantastic!

4. What kinds of books do you **not** enjoy reading? Why?

   I don't like to read scary novels because then I have trouble sleeping at night.

5. How has your interest in reading materials changed over time?

   To tell the truth, it hasn't changed at all over time.

Part 3 Write a book review below.

Comprehension Review

Fill in the best answer for each question.

_____ ❶ **If you wanted to read about an astronaut's point of view of space exploration, what could you read?**
- Ⓐ a book about the history of NASA
- Ⓑ a book about European explorers
- Ⓒ an astronaut's personal log
- Ⓓ an editorial about the Moon

_____ ❷ **This passage would not be a good choice if you wanted to _____**
- Ⓐ learn about Sputnik I.
- Ⓑ read about pollution on Earth.
- Ⓒ read about the International Space Station.
- Ⓓ find out NASA's plans for the future.

_____ ❸ **This passage would probably interest someone who likes _____**
- Ⓐ math.
- Ⓑ African history.
- Ⓒ mysteries.
- Ⓓ science.

_____ ❹ **Neil Armstrong said, "One small step for man, one giant leap for mankind."**
What does this mean?
- Ⓐ His accomplishment was important for people everywhere, then and in the future.
- Ⓑ He only took a small step on the Moon.
- Ⓒ He wanted all men to be able to walk on the Moon.
- Ⓓ His actions showed his kindness toward men.

_____ ❺ **In what way is the New Horizons spacecraft different from the International Space Station?**
- Ⓐ New Horizons is unmanned.
- Ⓑ New Horizons does not fly in space.
- Ⓒ New Horizons is one of the brightest objects in the night sky.
- Ⓓ Crew members stay on New Horizons about six months.

_____ ❻ **Which of these is not a first?**
- Ⓐ Yuri Gagarin became the first person to pilot a spacecraft.
- Ⓑ NASA was the first to develop a space station.
- Ⓒ Neil Armstrong was the first person to walk on the Moon.
- Ⓓ Pioneer 10 was the first manmade object to leave the solar system.

Word Power

Choose the English word from the Vocabulary list that correctly matches the definition.

 a manmade object that orbits Earth, the Moon, or another body in space

_____

 an astronaut working with the Soviet or Russian space program

_____

 a specific task given to a person or group

_____

 to send something out

_____

Jumpin' Johnny

Reading Tip

- Authors often use **vivid and rich vocabulary** as a strategy for describing characters.

- **Appealing to the five senses** by including descriptions that readers can almost see, smell, touch, hear, or taste is another strategy that authors frequently use.

Skill Overview

The main characters is often the focus of a story. Knowing how characters are developed (for example, through their **actions**, **physical descriptions**, and **character descriptions**) helps readers understand how stories work. This knowledge is useful whether the stories are being read or listened to.

Tall, skinny, **imposing**—that's how Johnny's friends would **describe** him. Johnny's blond hair was always spiked with a bit of gel so that it would stay in place all day. He wore the latest fashions: gigantic T-shirts, baggy shorts, and expensive athletic shoes. What the girls liked best, though, were his sparkling blue eyes that always suggested **mischief**.

Johnny was a powerhouse on the basketball court, too. Some say he could make a **shot** from a thousand feet away. His **agility** enabled him to leap, dodge, and dance down the basketball court.

In action, he was a gazelle, moving effortlessly toward his destination. On the court, his friends called him "Jumpin' Johnny." He earned this name because he would **soar** through the air about 10 feet, slam the ball into the net, and land on his feet. Then he would race down the court for the next play.

At home, Jumpin' Johnny was neither mischievous nor did he leap, jump, and dodge. He helped his little sister with homework. He also assisted with setting the dinner table and mowed the lawn every weekend during the summer. He loved history and would spend hours every evening reading about famous battles and former presidents of the United States. But when one of his friends called, Johnny once again **assumed** his school personality. He would talk, laughing and joking to show that he didn't take life too seriously. After all, he knew that the following day would bring more mischief and **adventure**.

Reading Skill Comprehension Practice

 **Hyperbole**

This means that an idea is **intentionally exaggerated** to create a strong impression.

For example, *make a shot from a thousand feet away*

 **Part 1** Record any descriptive words or phrases in the passage that helped you understand the character.

The following words and phrases from the passage helped me understand the character:

_____

_____

 **Part 2** Think about what you imagined as you read this passage. Then answer the questions below.

1. What did you **see** as you read this passage?

2. What did you **smell** as you read this passage?

3. What did you **hear** as you read this passage?

4. What did you **feel** as you read this passage?

 **Part 3** Write what you learned about Johnny from reading the author's description. Include words or phrases from the passage that describe Johnny.

_____

_____

_____

Comprehension Review

Fill in the best answer for each question.

❶ Which words describe Johnny?
Ⓐ athletic and friendly
Ⓑ shy and timid
Ⓒ lazy and selfish
Ⓓ clumsy and awkward

❷ Which would *not* be a good gift for Johnny?
Ⓐ a new basketball
Ⓑ a book about the presidents
Ⓒ a math book
Ⓓ a new T-shirt and a pair of baggy shorts

❸ Johnny would probably _____
Ⓐ wear a used pair of sneakers.
Ⓑ help a friend with homework.
Ⓒ throw away his history books.
Ⓓ skip a basketball game.

❹ Why does the author say that Johnny could make a shot from a thousand feet away?
Ⓐ because Johnny could really make a shot from a thousand feet away
Ⓑ to make fun of Johnny
Ⓒ to show how good a student Johnny was
Ⓓ to show what a good athlete Johnny was

❺ What is the purpose of this passage?
Ⓐ to describe the rules of basketball
Ⓑ to get you to play more sports
Ⓒ to describe Johnny
Ⓓ to give advice about being a good student

❻ Johnny's friends probably _____
Ⓐ like to play basketball.
Ⓑ do not think he is good at basketball.
Ⓒ do not think he is helpful.
Ⓓ think he is too shy.

Word Power

Choose the English word from the Vocabulary list that correctly matches the definition.

 to rise very quickly to a high level

 playful behavior that is thought of as somewhat naughty

 the ability to move easily and gracefully

 large in size

Reading Tip

- Follow the instruction in Part 1 before you listen to and read the passage.

- Different kinds of texts require different kinds of organizational structures. For example, a biography is typically written in chronological order.

Skill Overview

Authors structure, or organize, the information in their writing so that it makes sense to the reader. The structure of a text often depends on the topic; for example, instructions are usually presented in sequential order so they are logical and easy for readers to follow. Developing an awareness of the structure helps a reader to better understand a text.

Hydroponics

🎧 09

"Raising plants without dirt sounds like complete nonsense!" my Aunt Emma exclaimed in disbelief. "I've never seen a garden that didn't **contain** lots of good black soil."

"We learned all about it today in class," I explained. "It's called *hydroponics*—growing plants in water instead of soil—and people have been doing it for thousands of years. Look, here is a list of things you need and how to do it." I handed her the instructions that I'd gotten from my teacher that day. "I'm considering growing plants in a hydroponic **environment** for my science project this year. I'd **appreciate** it if you'd help me because you are an expert at growing things!"

A hydroponic farm

Things you need:

- wide-mouthed jar
- piece of cotton rope
- vermiculite
- foam cup
- seeds
- hydroponic **fertilizer**

How to do it:

1. Cut a piece of rope as long as the height of the jar. **Fray** both ends of the rope in order to create your wick.

2. Poke a hole in the bottom of the cup. Insert the rope through the hole in the cup and hold it there while you fill the cup with vermiculite.

3. Create an **effective** plant nutrient by mixing hydroponic fertilizer with water.

4. Fill the jar with just enough plant nutrient water so that it will not touch the bottom of the cup once the cup is **inserted** into the neck of the jar.

5. Insert the foam cup into the neck of the jar so that the wick hangs down in the plant nutrient water.

6. Plant your seeds in the vermiculite (not too deep).

7. Place your pot where it will **receive** a lot of sunlight.

My aunt did help me with my science project. One day she said, "You know, the only thing wrong with hydroponic gardening is that your hands don't get dirty!"

Vocabulary

contain
to have something inside

environment
the air, water, and land in or on which people, animals, and plants live

appreciate
to recognize and value how good someone or something is

fertilizer
a substance used to produce larger, healthier plant life

✪**fray**
to separate the threads at the edge of a fabric or cloth

effective
producing the desired result; working well

insert
to put something inside something else

receive
to get or be given something

Reading Skill Comprehension Practice

 **1** Describe your experience following a set of directions, or think about something that comes with a set of directions and write about it below.

_____

_____

_____

 **2** Use the passage to answer the following questions about growing plants with hydroponics.

1. How long have people been using hydroponics to grow plants?

_____

2. Where should you place your plant pot?

_____

3. What makes hydroponic gardening so unusual?

_____

4. How should you plant your seeds in the vermiculite?

_____

Part 3 Match the text description on the left with the appropriate organizational structure on the right. Some of the organizational structures may be used more than once.

Texts	Organizational Structures
_____ **1.** a dictionary	**A.** similar items are grouped together
_____ **2.** a history book about the Civil War	**B.** alphabetical order
_____ **3.** a catalog of toys, clothes, and books	**C.** compare and contrast
_____ **4.** a directions for putting together a model plane	**D.** sequential order
_____ **5.** a book about Mars and Earth	**E.** chronological order
_____ **6.** an encyclopedia	**F.** proposition and support
_____ **7.** a letter to the editor	
_____ **8.** an article about holidays around the world	
_____ **9.** a biography of Rosa Parks	
_____ **10.** a recipe	

Comprehension Review

Fill in the best answer for each question.

❶ When should you mix hydroponic fertilizer with water?
ⓐ after you plant the seeds
ⓑ before you pour the water into the jar
ⓒ while you are fraying the rope
ⓓ after you place your plant in the sunlight

❷ The foam cup is placed in the neck of the jar *after* _____
ⓐ the seeds are planted.
ⓑ the pot is placed in the sunlight.
ⓒ the wick hangs down into the plant nutrient.
ⓓ the jar is filled with plant nutrient.

❸ What is the *first* step in making a hydroponic garden?
ⓐ Plant the seeds.
ⓑ Fill the jar with plant nutrients.
ⓒ Gather the materials you will need.
ⓓ Hang the wick upside down in the plant nutrient.

❹ In hydroponics, vermiculite is used instead of _____
ⓐ dirt.
ⓑ seeds.
ⓒ water.
ⓓ a pot.

❺ Why did the author ask Aunt Emma for help?
ⓐ Aunt Emma knows all about hydroponics.
ⓑ Aunt Emma is an expert at growing things.
ⓒ Aunt Emma is a science teacher.
ⓓ Aunt Emma doesn't like to get her hands dirty.

❻ Why is it important for the rope to hang down into the plant nutrient?
ⓐ to get nutrients to the plant
ⓑ to get sunlight to the plant
ⓒ to get vermiculite to the plant
ⓓ to get dirt to the plant

Word Power

Choose the English word from the Vocabulary list that correctly matches the definition.

 to separate the threads at the edge of a fabric or cloth

 a substance used to produce larger, healthier plant life

 producing the desired result; working well

 to put something inside something else

39

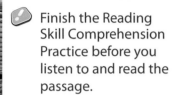

Reading Tip

Finish the Reading Skill Comprehension Practice before you listen to and read the passage.

One way to make sense of a heading is to turn it into a question, and then read the passage to find the answer to the question.

Benjamin Franklin,
The Death of a Great Man

Skill Overview

Headings help readers determine the main idea and locate information in a text. Often, headings state the topic in a single word or short phrase. Learning to recognize headings and using them consistently will help readers to increase reading comprehension.

Five-man drafting committee of the Declaration of Independence presenting its work to Congress

Franklin's Return to Philadelphia, 1785

10

Benjamin Franklin died on April 17, 1790. In his 1738 *Poor Richard's Almanack*, Franklin had written, "If you wou'd not be forgotten as soon as you are dead and rotten, either write things worth reading, or do things worth the writing." Franklin truly **fulfilled** this **statement**. He was a great writer, and he was a great doer.

A Writer

When Franklin was young, his funny letters to the editor made the town newspaper a hit. He made his almanac a best seller by predicting the death of his competitor. Even though his competitor did not die, the townspeople loved it! But Franklin wasn't just a **creative** writer. He helped write the two most important **documents** in United States history. One of them was the Declaration of Independence. The other was the U.S. Constitution.

A Politician

Franklin was also a skilled politician. People in Philadelphia chose him to **represent** them in the British Parliament. Soon after, other colonies chose him as their **diplomat**, too. Returning home, he supported the colonies in the Revolutionary War. Then, the U.S. Congress sent him to France. The French loved Franklin and treated him like a celebrity. Because of Franklin, the French helped the colonies win the war. At the end of the war, he even worked to **negotiate** peace with England.

Serving His Country

Franklin was more than a writer and a politician. He studied electricity, formed a library, and built a hospital. Franklin also began the first fire department and police force in Philadelphia. In so many ways, he served his country well.

Vocabulary

✪almanack
alternative spelling for *almanac*—a book containing calendars and facts about the rising and setting of the Sun and Moon, tide changes, etc.

fulfill
to accomplish or satisfy; to complete

statement
something that someone says or writes officially, or an action done to express an opinion

creative
producing or using original and unusual ideas

document
a paper or set of papers with written or printed information

represent
to speak, act, or be present officially for another person or people

diplomat
a person who works to keep peace between countries

negotiate
to have formal discussions with someone in order to reach an agreement with him or her

41

Reading Skill Comprehension Practice

Part 1 Explain why an author might include headings in a story or book.

Headings might be included to _____

_____

_____

Part 2 Think about what you might read about in a passage titled Benjamin Franklin, The Death of a Great Man. Write your prediction.

I might read about _____

_____

_____

_____

Part 3 Use each heading to form a question about the text, and then predict the answer.

A Writer

Question:

_____

_____

Predicted answer:

_____

_____

A Politician

Question:

_____

_____

Predicted answer:

_____

_____

Serving His Country

Question:

_____

_____

Predicted answer:

_____

_____

Comprehension Review

Fill in the best answer for each question.

_____ **1** What would be another good title for this passage?

Ⓐ Poor Richard's Almanack

Ⓑ Benjamin Franklin, Writer

Ⓒ The Accomplishments of Benjamin Franklin

Ⓓ Franklin's Early Life

_____ **2** The title tells you that this passage is *mostly* about _____

Ⓐ the first fire department.

Ⓑ what made Benjamin Franklin an important person.

Ⓒ how Franklin wrote *Poor Richard's Almanack*.

Ⓓ Franklin's experiments with electricity.

_____ **3** Which of these is a detail supporting the main idea?

Ⓐ Franklin was born in Boston.

Ⓑ Franklin was originally going to be a printer.

Ⓒ Franklin went to Philadelphia at the age of 17.

Ⓓ Franklin helped to write the U.S. Constitution.

_____ **4** What did Franklin suggest to people who want to be remembered?

Ⓐ Write things worth reading, or do things worth writing about.

Ⓑ Design new inventions.

Ⓒ Become a writer.

Ⓓ Study electricity and other sciences.

_____ **5** The author would probably agree with which statement?

Ⓐ Benjamin Franklin was not an important American.

Ⓑ Benjamin Franklin should be remembered.

Ⓒ Benjamin Franklin accomplished very little in his life.

Ⓓ Benjamin Franklin did not write very well.

_____ **6** Which of these was *not* one of Franklin's accomplishments?

Ⓐ building a hospital

Ⓑ forming a library

Ⓒ beginning a fire department

Ⓓ becoming president of the United States

Word Power

Choose the English word from the Vocabulary list that correctly matches the definition.

1 a paper or set of papers with written or printed information

_____

2 a person who works to keep peace between countries

_____

3 to accomplish or satisfy; to complete

_____

4 alternative spelling for *almanac*—a book containing calendars and facts about the rising and setting of the Sun and Moon, tide changes, etc.

_____

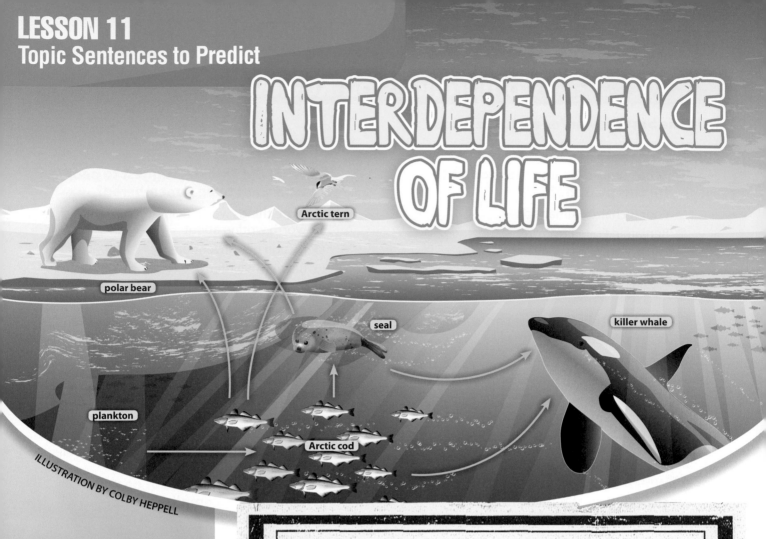

INTERDEPENDENCE OF LIFE

Arctic tern

polar bear

seal

killer whale

plankton

Arctic cod

ILLUSTRATION BY COLBY HEPPELL

Reading Tip

- Follow the instruction in Part 1 before you listen to and read the passage.

- Sometimes you have to revise your prediction about a text. This is a strategy to help you stay focused on your reading.

Skill Overview

A **topic sentence** is a general sentence that expresses the main idea of a paragraph. It is usually the first or last sentence in the paragraph and is followed by supporting sentences. Readers should recognize how topic sentences can help them make meaningful predictions about the content of a text.

 11

Green plants are called *producers* in the chain of life. They use carbon dioxide, water, minerals, and sunlight to **produce** their own food. The food that they produce is a simple form of sugar, which gives them energy to grow.

During this process, called ***photosynthesis***, the plant **releases** oxygen and water through its leaves. Producers are important because they produce food not only for themselves, but also for others.

Consumers are the living organisms that get energy from eating others. Animals may eat plants or other animals to **obtain** energy to maintain life. Decomposers are organisms that help break down dead organisms or their parts. Decomposers break down leaves, wood, and animals and help the cycle of life continue.

In a **community**, organisms live together and pass energy on to one another. This is called the *food chain*. For example, a plant is eaten by an insect, which is eaten by a bird. The bird is eaten by a snake, which is then eaten by a hawk.

Food chains form food webs. A plant or animal in a food chain might also be linked to another part of the food web. For example, the insect might also be a part of a food chain for a frog and a snake. There are many links that make up a food web in a community.

Energy for life is available to organisms at each level of the feeding order. The producers, or green plants, have the most energy. They use some of the energy for themselves. They need the energy to grow and perform photosynthesis. Some of the energy is passed along to others when plants are eaten. The animal that eats the plant gets energy from this food. The energy can be used to help that animal stay alive and function. The energy that is contained in the animal is passed on to other consumers when the animal is eaten. This chain of life takes on the form of a **pyramid**, with the most energy available at the bottom and the least amount of energy at the top of the pyramid.

People have an effect on food chains and food webs. When a forest is cleared, for example, both producers and consumers are affected. The wood comes from a tree, which is a producer. Within the forest are other consumers and producers that may be linked to that tree for their needs. Clearing land to build new cities or highways can be destructive to the community of life that once lived there.

✪**interdependence**
the state of having many organisms depend on one another

produce
to make something or bring something into existence

✪**photosynthesis**
the process plants use to produce energy

release
to give freedom or free movement to someone or something

consumer
an organism that eats another organism

obtain
to get something

community
the organisms living in one particular area

pyramid
a solid object with a square base and four triangular sides that form a point at the top

A food chain

Reading Skill Comprehension Practice

Part 1 Make a prediction about the passage based on the following topic sentence, which was taken from the text.

Topic Sentence

In a community, organisms live together and pass energy on to each other.

My Prediction

_____

Part 2 After you read the passage, summarize what it is actually about.

What the Passage Is About

_____
_____

Part 3 List two additional topic sentences from the passage.

1. In a community, organisms live together and pass energy on to each other.

2. _____
_____
_____

3. _____
_____
_____

Comprehension Review

Fill in the best answer for each question.

_____ ❶ *In a community, organisms live together and pass energy on to one another.*

This topic sentence tells you that the paragraph will be about _____

Ⓐ how organisms are connected.

Ⓑ the definition of community.

Ⓒ where most organisms live.

Ⓓ the difference between energy and food.

_____ ❷ **Which of these is the topic sentence of the first paragraph?**

Ⓐ The food that they produce is a simple form of sugar, which gives them energy to grow.

Ⓑ They use carbon dioxide, water, minerals, and sunlight to produce their own food.

Ⓒ Green plants are called *producers* in the chain of life.

Ⓓ Animals may eat plants or other animals to obtain energy to maintain life.

_____ ❸ *Food chains form food webs.*

Which statement is *not* a good prediction based on this topic sentence?

Ⓐ The paragraph will be about how food chains become food webs.

Ⓑ The paragraph will be about three kinds of foods.

Ⓒ The paragraph will be about how food chains are connected.

Ⓓ The paragraph will probably give examples of food webs.

_____ ❹ **According to the passage, how does clearing the land destroy the community of life?**

Ⓐ It removes producers, which are important to the food web.

Ⓑ It puts dangerous waste into the environment.

Ⓒ It ruins the soil.

Ⓓ It often starts forest fires.

_____ ❺ **Which is an example of a producer?**

Ⓐ a bird

Ⓑ a rabbit

Ⓒ a hawk

Ⓓ a tree

_____ ❻ **Why do you think food chains linked together are called *food webs*?**

Ⓐ They are mostly made of spiders.

Ⓑ They are made of producers, consumers, and decomposers.

Ⓒ They are linked together like the strands of a spider's web.

Ⓓ They can be ruined by clearing land.

Word Power

Choose the English word from the Vocabulary list that correctly matches the definition.

 an organism that eats another organism

_____

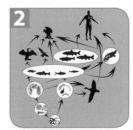 the state of having many organisms depend on one another

_____

 the process plants use to produce energy

_____

 to give freedom or free movement to someone or something

_____

Reading Tip

After you listen to and read the first paragraph, stop and follow the instruction in Part 1. Then finish the passage.

Skill Overview

Literary devices are specific aspects of writing that help readers understand and decide meaning in a text. These include **personification**, **simile**, **metaphor**, **alliteration**, and **tone**.

CITY SUMMER

Imagine a hot summer day. The Sun beats down on the blacktop, and the city air rises up in a zigzag. Light **bounces** off the cars parked on the street. For a time, the only sound heard throughout the neighborhood is the **steady** hum of fans, **laboring** to cool residents from the **sweltering** temperatures.

Bored children decide to brave the humid heat and play ball in the streets. Thump! Thump! Thump! The repetitive sound of a basketball breaks the **monotonous** silence. The children weave in and out, in and out, jumping, running, dodging, and laughing as they move effortlessly, making plays in the hot summer rays.

Spewing a nerve-jangling tune, an ice cream truck arrives on the scene. The kids race excitedly over to the truck and select treats—vanilla cones, chocolate crunch bars, wildly colored ice pops. Within minutes, the treats are **devoured**, and the kids return to their energetic play.

Dark storm clouds roll ominously through the sky overhead, and the street empties. A **gloomy** grayness envelops the sky like a giant umbrella. Craaack! Thunder roars with anger after lightning dances fleetingly in the distance. The rain comes in torrents, beating, beating, beating down on the sidewalks, streets, and houses. Faces peer curiously out windows, observing the dazzling show. When the clouds roll away, steam rises, drying the streets for another round of play.

Vocabulary

imagine
to form or have a mental picture or idea of something

bounce
to move up or away after hitting a surface

steady
happening in a smooth, gradual, and regular way

labor
to work hard

⭐**sweltering**
extremely hot

monotonous
having the same sound or tone

devour
to eat very quickly

gloomy
unhappy and without hope

49

Onomatopoeia

Words that imitate the sound associated with the thing in question

They give the reader more information about what something sounds like in a story.

Personification

Describing something non-human as if it were human

It allows the author to describe things in a more vivid, detailed way.

Part 1 Write what you were thinking about or imagining as you listened to and read the first paragraph.

_____

_____

Part 2 The author of the passage uses onomatopoeia to help convey certain images to readers. Write your own examples of onomatopoeia below.

Thump!	Craaak!	

Part 3 Find examples of personification in the passage. Write them below.

1. Thunder roars with anger; lightning dances fleetingly.

2. _____

3. _____

4. _____

Comprehension Review

Fill in the best answer for each question.

_____ ❶ **Which of these is a simile?**
- Ⓐ Bored children decided to brave the humid heat and play ball in the streets.
- Ⓑ A gloomy grayness envelops the sky like a giant umbrella.
- Ⓒ Faces peer curiously out windows, observing the dazzling show.
- Ⓓ Imagine a hot, summer day.

_____ ❷ *Gloomy grayness* **is an example of** _____
- Ⓐ a simile.
- Ⓑ a metaphor.
- Ⓒ repetition.
- Ⓓ alliteration.

_____ ❸ **Which literary device is** *not* **used in this passage?**
- Ⓐ alliteration
- Ⓑ simile
- Ⓒ metaphor
- Ⓓ repetition

_____ ❹ **What is the author's purpose?**
- Ⓐ to describe a hot summer day in the city
- Ⓑ to explain how to get around in a city
- Ⓒ to get you to visit a city
- Ⓓ to explain how cities developed

_____ ❺ **The author describes** *"the steady hum of fans."*

What does the word <u>hum</u> **mean in the phrase above?**
- Ⓐ singing without words
- Ⓑ a low, continuous noise
- Ⓒ a loud crash
- Ⓓ a musical tone

_____ ❻ **The children in this passage are probably** _____
- Ⓐ very chilly.
- Ⓑ in school.
- Ⓒ on summer vacation.
- Ⓓ inside.

Word Power

Choose the English word from the Vocabulary list that correctly matches the definition.

1  to eat very quickly

_____

2  extremely hot

_____

3  having the same sound or tone

_____

4  to work hard

_____

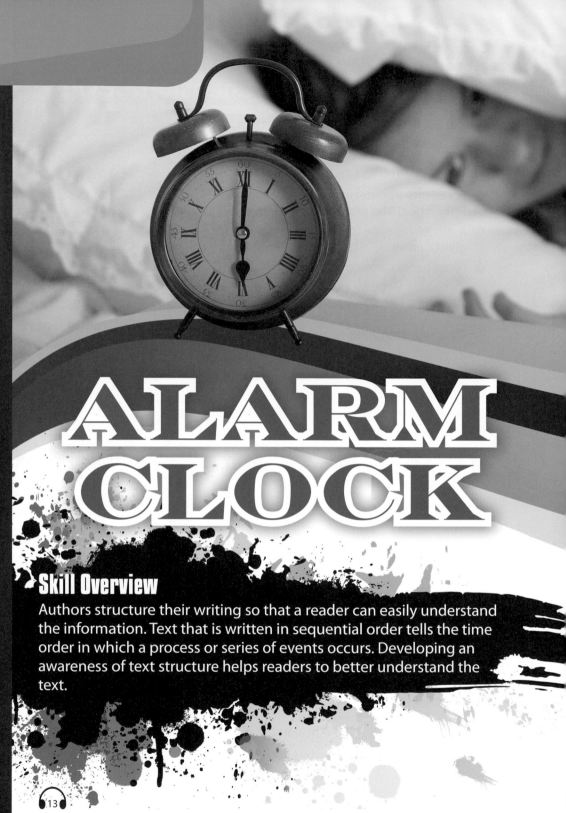

ALARM CLOCK

Skill Overview

Authors structure their writing so that a reader can easily understand the information. Text that is written in sequential order tells the time order in which a process or series of events occurs. Developing an awareness of text structure helps readers to better understand the text.

Awaking to the sound of the alarm, I knew I would be on my way to school shortly. Across the room, the alarm clock was still ringing. I stood on the floor beside my bed, rubbed my eyes, and then blindly stumbled over to the alarm. As I **clumsily** reached for the alarm, I noticed a **tingly sensation** in my hands and realized that I had no feeling in either one. Both of my hands had been folded under me while I slept through the night. Now, neither of my hands would move in any direction. I tried hitting the alarm with my heavy hands, but the alarm continued ringing. Both the left hand and the right hand did the exact same thing—absolutely nothing!

Vocabulary

clumsily
in an awkward way

⊗**tingly**
prickling or thrilling

sensation
the ability to feel something physically

hysterically
with an extreme outburst of emotion

collapse
to fall down suddenly

attempt
to try to do something

surrender
to stop fighting and admit defeat

⊗**resounding**
loud

Now laughing **hysterically**, I leaned over the alarm and pressed on the button with my nose. My nose didn't fit in the small area. I tried the same with my elbow, but it was also too large. I tried sitting on it, with no results. I **collapsed** on the bed, lifted my foot into the air, and **attempted** to use my toe to poke at the button. Nothing worked, and the alarm rang on.

I **surrendered** to the sound and decided to wait. I shuffled through the hallway and into the kitchen, as the **resounding** noise of that alarm rang through the house. Then the feeling slowly began returning to my hands. I sprinted down the hallway, up the steps, and back into the bedroom and anxiously pushed on the button.

The silence was fabulous! I know from past experience that when your day begins this way, you should just go back to bed. That's exactly what I did. As I fell back asleep, I realized that the alarm ringing for so long was even worse than I had thought—because it was Saturday!

Reading Skill Comprehension Practice

Part 1 Think about why the narrator chose to tell the story in sequential order. Write your ideas below.

The narrator told this in chronological order because _____

_____

_____

Part 2 List any words or phrases that indicate this passage is written in sequential order.

_____   _____   _____

Part 3 On the time line below, show the events that happened in the ALARM CLOCK passage.

_____   _____
_____   _____

1   **2**   **3**   **4**

_____   _____
_____   _____

Comprehension Review

Fill in the best answer for each question.

_____ **1 Which event happened *first*?**
- Ⓐ The alarm clock rang.
- Ⓑ The narrator felt a tingly sensation in both hands.
- Ⓒ The narrator fell back to sleep.
- Ⓓ The narrator realized it was Saturday.

_____ **2 In which order did the narrator use different body parts to try turning off the alarm clock?**
- Ⓐ nose, hands, elbow
- Ⓑ elbow, hands, toe
- Ⓒ hands, nose, elbow
- Ⓓ elbow, nose, toe

_____ **3 Which list is in the right order?**
- Ⓐ I fell back to sleep. The alarm clock rang. I sprinted up the stairs.
- Ⓑ I had no feeling in my hands. I pressed on the button with my nose. The silence was fabulous.
- Ⓒ I shuffled through the hallway. I stood up. I sat on the alarm clock.
- Ⓓ I realized it was Saturday. I rubbed my eyes. My nose didn't fit on the alarm clock button.

_____ **4 At the end of the story, how did the narrator probably feel?**
- Ⓐ tired
- Ⓑ shy
- Ⓒ excited
- Ⓓ lonely

_____ **5 The narrator's hands had no feeling from _____**
- Ⓐ hitting the alarm clock too much.
- Ⓑ falling down the stairs.
- Ⓒ an illness.
- Ⓓ being folded under her all night.

_____ **6 What happened after the narrator tried sitting on the alarm clock?**
- Ⓐ The alarm clock turned off.
- Ⓑ The alarm clock kept ringing, so she tried using a toe.
- Ⓒ The alarm clock kept ringing, so she tried using an elbow.
- Ⓓ The alarm clock broke.

Word Power

Choose the English word from the Vocabulary list that correctly matches the definition.

 prickling or thrilling

_____

 loud

_____

 to stop fighting and admit defeat

_____

 with an extreme outburst of emotion

_____

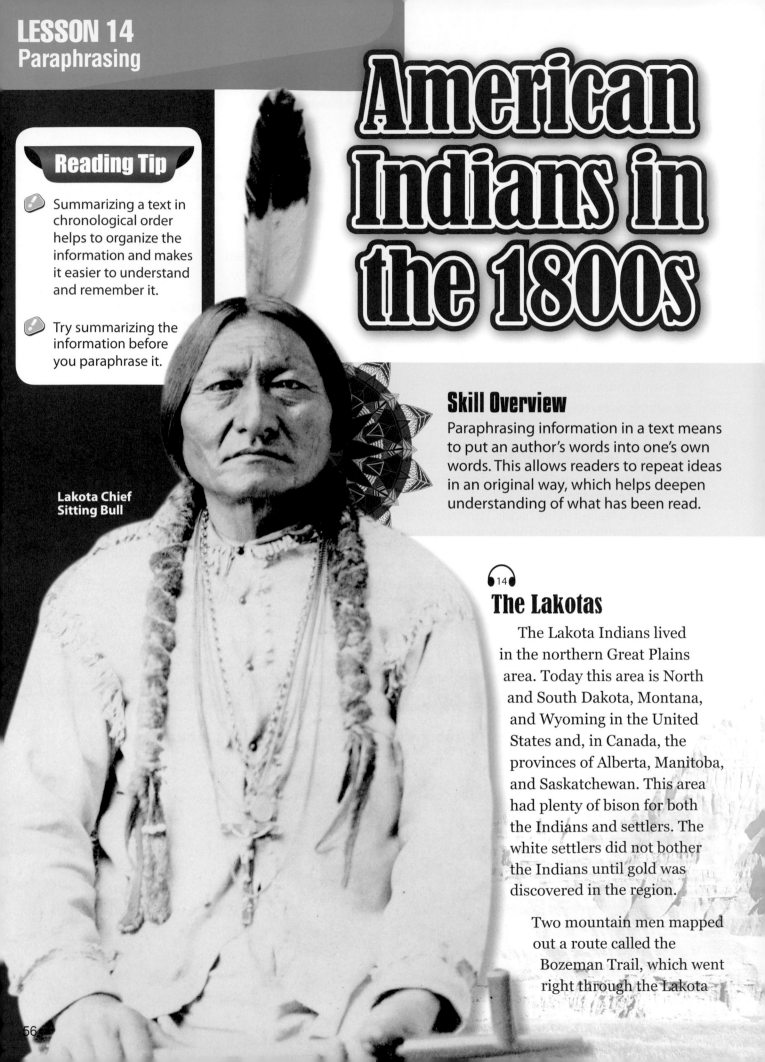

American Indians in the 1800s

Lakota Chief Sitting Bull

Skill Overview

Paraphrasing information in a text means to put an author's words into one's own words. This allows readers to repeat ideas in an original way, which helps deepen understanding of what has been read.

The Lakotas

The Lakota Indians lived in the northern Great Plains area. Today this area is North and South Dakota, Montana, and Wyoming in the United States and, in Canada, the provinces of Alberta, Manitoba, and Saskatchewan. This area had plenty of bison for both the Indians and settlers. The white settlers did not bother the Indians until gold was discovered in the region.

Two mountain men mapped out a route called the Bozeman Trail, which went right through the Lakota

territory. Gold miners began traveling the route in large numbers.

Lakota Sioux chiefs

A Lakota chief named Red Cloud wanted the Bozeman Trail closed. Miners and wagons **disturbed** the bison. Hunting became more difficult. The Lakota began to threaten everyone who used the trail. The travelers asked for government **protection**.

U.S. government **officials** knew they had to do something. They did not want the miners to be attacked along the trail. The government met with Red Cloud and other chiefs to find a solution. During the meeting, Red Cloud noticed army troops on the trail. The troops were building forts. Red Cloud realized the meeting did not really matter. The government planned to keep the trail open. He was furious!

The Lakota bands joined together and attacked the forts. Many soldiers were killed. The government found it too hard to protect the trail. The army left, and the Lakota burned down the forts. This was an important victory for Red Cloud and his people.

After Red Cloud's War, a **treaty** was signed at Fort Laramie. The government closed the Bozeman Trail. A large piece of land was set aside for Lakota tribes in the Dakota Territory. This land included the sacred Black Hills. The Lakota believed the Black Hills were the birthplace of their tribe.

In 1874, gold was found in the Black Hills. The Lakota were upset when miners from all over the country **invaded** their **sacred** land. The Lakota attacked those who entered the Black Hills. The government offered to buy the Black Hills, but the Lakota refused to sell.

The Lakota chief, Sitting Bull, moved his band to its summer camp along the Little Bighorn River. There were Cheyenne Indians in camp as well. The U.S. Army sent troops to force them back to the **reservation**.

General George Custer was famous from his years fighting in the Civil War. Marching his troops hard, he led an attack against the Lakota Indians. There were many more Indians than Custer expected. In the end, General Custer and his men lost the battle and their lives.

Vocabulary

territory
land, or sometimes sea, that is thought to belong to or be connected with a particular country

disturb
to interrupt

protection
the act of protecting or the state of being protected

official
a person with authority in a government or a company

treaty
a written agreement between two or more countries, formally approved and signed by their leaders

invade
to enter a place by force in order to take possession of it

sacred
highly valued

reservation
an area of land set aside for a specific purpose

Bison

57

Reading Skill Comprehension Practice

Summarize

It means to express the most important facts or ideas about something or someone **in a short and clear form**.

Paraphrase

It is much like summarizing. However, to *paraphrase* means to describe the most essential points **in one's own words**.

Part 1 Review the passage and think about the beginning, middle, and end. Write a **summary** for each part of the passage.

Summary of the **beginning** of the passage: _____
_____

Summary of the **middle** of the passage: _____
_____

Summary of the **end** of the passage: _____
_____

Part 2 **Paraphrase** the information from the passage. Remember to use your own words.

_____
_____
_____
_____
_____

Comprehension Review

Fill in the best answer for each question.

❶ Which statement is a good paraphrase of the first two sentences of the passage?

Ⓐ The Lakota Indians lived in the area that is now south central Canada and north central United States.

Ⓑ The Lakota Indians lived in North and South Dakota.

Ⓒ The Lakota Indians lived in Canada.

Ⓓ The Lakota Indians hunted bison.

❷ Which sentence best summarizes the information about the treaty signed at Fort Laramie?

Ⓐ The treaty closed the Bozeman Trail and set aside land in Dakota Territory for the Lakota.

Ⓑ The treaty closed the Bozeman Trail and opened up gold mines in the Black Hills.

Ⓒ The Lakota bands gathered together and burned Fort Laramie.

Ⓓ A treaty was signed at Fort Laramie.

❸ If someone asked you what this passage is about, what should you say?

Ⓐ the wars and treaties between the Lakota Indians and white settlers

Ⓑ the way that the Lakota Indians lived long ago

Ⓒ how U.S. officials protected white settlers on the Bozeman Trail

Ⓓ how the Lakota Indians opened the Bozeman Trail to white settlers

❹ What is a bison?

Ⓐ a type of gold

Ⓑ a gold miner

Ⓒ tent that Lakota Indians used

Ⓓ an of animal that Lakota Indians hunted

❺ Why did miners come to the Black Hills in the Dakota territory?

Ⓐ Gold had been discovered there.

Ⓑ Bison had been discovered there.

Ⓒ They believed the Black Hills were sacred.

Ⓓ The government forced them to move there.

❻ What happened when General Custer led his troops against Sitting Bull and his band?

Ⓐ The U.S. government won the battle.

Ⓑ General Custer sided with the Indians.

Ⓒ The Bozeman Trail was closed.

Ⓓ General Custer and his troops lost their lives.

Word Power

Choose the English word from the Vocabulary list that correctly matches the definition.

 1 highly valued

 2 an area of land set aside for a specific purpose

 3 a person with authority in a government or a company

 4 to enter a place by force in order to take possession of it

Who Were Abolitionists?

Reading Tip

Listen to and read the passage up to the last paragraph. Then follow the instruction in Part 1 before you finish the passage.

Skill Overview

A summary sentence summarizes the information in a passage, usually in a single sentence. Summary sentences are typically the last sentence in a passage or paragraph. Effective readers are able to use summary sentences to determine the main idea and locate information.

15

When the U.S. Constitution was written in 1787, the leaders of the country **debated** slavery. Southern leaders **convinced** the others to keep slavery legal. Soon after, leaders of the churches began to ask if slavery was right. The first group of people to speak out against slavery was the Quakers. They wanted to end all slavery in America.

By the early 1800s, life was changing in the United States. People in the northern and middle states were not using slaves anymore. However, the southern states **refused** to end slavery. Many people thought the South should be **forced** to stop slavery. These people were called *abolitionists*. They thought all slaves should be free.

Abolitionists knew that they would face a fight in the South. Southerners would not want to end slavery. Most people believed that slave trading and slave auctions were the worst part of slavery. Abolitionists decided to attack that part of slavery first. After a long debate, it was decided that all slave trade in the United States must end by 1807.

The Underground Railroad

Some slaves tried to escape from their owners. Most were caught and punished. A few were even killed. Escaping became a little easier when abolitionists started to help. They organized an **escape route** from the South to the northern states and Canada. They called this route the "Underground Railroad."

The Underground Railroad did not have train tracks like a normal railroad. It was a "railroad" because it had many stops on the way to freedom. It was "underground" because it was a secret. A person who led a group to freedom on the Underground Railroad was a conductor. The slaves who traveled the railroad were passengers.

If a slave wanted to escape, he or she would be contacted by an abolitionist in the South. This person would tell the slave where to go for the first stop on the route to the North. At each stop along the way, the escaping slave would be told where the next stop was. Sometimes, slaves had to hide in trees, **swamps**, or barns. Often, slave catchers were chasing after them.

Some abolitionists just provided information. Others hid slaves in their homes and fed and clothed them. A few acted as conductors. All these people **risked** their lives to help others gain their freedom.

Vocabulary

debate
to discuss or examine from different viewpoints

convince
to persuade someone or cause someone to believe something

refuse
to say you will not do or accept something

force
to make someone do something against his or her wishes

escape
to get free from something

route
a course of travel

swamp
wet, spongy land often partly covered with water

risk
to do something despite the chance of a bad result

Reading Skill Comprehension Practice

 **Part 1** Write three facts about the abolitionists from this passage.

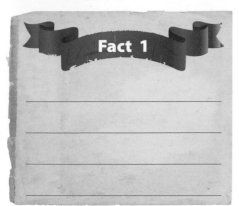
Fact 1
_____
_____
_____

Fact 2
_____
_____
_____

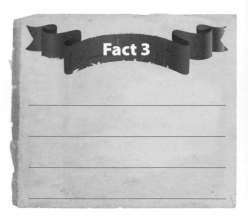
Fact 3
_____
_____
_____

 **Part 2** Now that you have read the entire passage about the abolitionists, answer the questions below.

1. What are your opinions about abolitionists now?

_____

2. Is your reaction different now that you have read the summary sentence?

_____

 **Part 3** Write the author's main idea, or central message, in this story.

_____

_____

_____

Comprehension Review

Fill in the best answer for each question.

_____ ❶ **Which sentence correctly summarizes the last paragraph?**

Ⓐ Some abolitionists just provided information.

Ⓑ All these people risked their lives to help others gain their freedom.

Ⓒ A few acted as conductors.

Ⓓ A person who led a group to freedom on the Underground Railroad was a conductor.

_____ ❷ **What is the main idea of the first paragraph?**

Ⓐ Leaders of the country debated whether slavery was right.

Ⓑ Quakers wanted to end slavery.

Ⓒ Southern leaders wanted to keep slavery.

Ⓓ The Constitution of the United States ended slavery.

_____ ❸ **The summary sentence in the last paragraph tells you that the** _most_ **important information is** _____

Ⓐ how and why abolitionists helped slaves escape.

Ⓑ that slaves on the Underground Railroad were called _passengers_.

Ⓒ that slavery was debated by many people.

Ⓓ that the Underground Railroad was kept secret.

_____ ❹ **In the phrase** _Underground Railroad,_ **what does the word** _underground_ **mean?**

Ⓐ beneath the earth

Ⓑ below the sea

Ⓒ buried

Ⓓ secret

_____ ❺ **Why did people likely use words up to** _passengers_ **and** _conductors_ **instead of** _slaves_ **and** _abolitionists_?

Ⓐ Nobody knew about abolitionists.

Ⓑ Abolitionists and slaves did not want to get caught.

Ⓒ Most people could not read well and did not know those words.

Ⓓ Railroads were used to move slaves from the South to the North.

_____ ❻ **Which sentence is true?**

Ⓐ Helping slaves to escape was very dangerous.

Ⓑ Most people supported slavery.

Ⓒ Abolitionists wanted to keep slavery, especially in the South.

Ⓓ Almost everyone thought the abolitionists were right.

Word Power

Choose the English word from the Vocabulary list that correctly matches the definition.

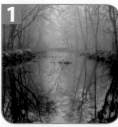 1

wet, spongy land often partly covered with water

_____

 2

a course of travel

_____

 3

to make someone do something against his or her wishes

_____

 4

to discuss or examine from different viewpoints

_____

ARCHITECTURAL SHAPES

Skill Overview

Readers reflect on text when they think about what they are reading and form ideas about it. Reflecting helps readers make sense of a text and connect it with what they already know.

🎧 16

Wade's family is going to build a new house on a plot of land. The neighborhood is a great place for Wade's family to live because Wade's parents work close by, and his friends live in the area.

Fallingwater

Wade wonders what their new house will look like. He begins to look at many kinds of homes and notices several different shapes in the houses' **designs**.

If you carefully study the apartments or houses in your neighborhood, you will **recognize** many shapes. The study of shapes is called *geometry*. Geometry is all around us.

Architects design buildings. Wade's family meets with an architect. They discuss what their house will look like. Then the architect shows Wade's family a picture of his favorite building—a fire station.

Architects choose the shapes that make up a building and its rooms. Consider your own house or apartment. It is **composed** of many three-dimensional shapes. Rectangular prisms and cubes are good three-dimensional shapes for rooms.

The family's architect talks about where the rooms should be built. Bedrooms, which are for sleeping, should be away from noisy rooms, such as the kitchen. The architect shows Wade and his family some pictures of amazing houses. Wade's family looks closely at the photos to get ideas. Wade notices that the **wooden** beams and **brick** columns in one house are shaped like rectangular prisms. Wade sees that each roof for this house looks like a **flat** rectangular prism. He also reads about a famous house called "Fallingwater."

After the family has shared all of its ideas, the architect draws a plan showing what the house will look like when it is built.

Vocabulary

design
the way something has been made or put together

recognize
to know someone or something because you have seen, heard, or experienced it before

geometry
an area of math that deals with points, lines, shapes, etc.

architect
a person who designs homes and buildings

composed
formed; made with

wooden
made of wood

A wooden spoon

brick
a rectangular block of hard material

flat
level and smooth

Reading Skill Comprehension Practice

 **Write down any thoughts or opinions you formed while reading this passage.**

1. I think it would be thrilling if we can actually build our home from scratch one day!

2. _____

_____

_____

 **Think about how this passage is related to your own life. Write your personal response below.**

1. I can relate to this passage because my family just bought a new house, and we have spent a lot of time discussing the interior of the home.

2. _____

_____

_____

Part 3 **Read the passage again, and then write a sentence or two about your dream house.**

1. My dream home would be made of wood and would have a room with walls of bookshelves to store my books.

2. _____

_____

_____

Comprehension Review

Fill in the best answer for each question.

_____ ❶ **Which is the best way to reflect on the author's description of how shapes are used in buildings?**

Ⓐ by drawing different kinds of shapes

Ⓑ by asking an architect

Ⓒ by thinking about the shapes and rooms in your own home

Ⓓ by taking a geometry class

_____ ❷ **What happens when a bedroom is next to the kitchen in a house?**

Ⓐ People can sleep better.

Ⓑ It is probably too noisy to sleep.

Ⓒ It is easier to watch TV.

Ⓓ More people want to buy the house.

_____ ❸ **How does looking at houses and rooms help you think about geometry?**

Ⓐ They are made of shapes, and geometry is the study of shapes.

Ⓑ Architects study geometry.

Ⓒ Most buildings are made of circular shapes.

Ⓓ An architect designs buildings.

_____ ❹ **Wade's family is going to build a new house on a plot of land.**

What does _plot_ mean in this sentence?

Ⓐ the events in a story

Ⓑ a kind of building

Ⓒ a piece of land

Ⓓ a kind of shape

_____ ❺ **Why does the author say, "Geometry is all around us"?**

Ⓐ There are many architects.

Ⓑ Wade's family will live close to where his parents work.

Ⓒ Geometry is the study of shapes.

Ⓓ Many things are made of shapes, and geometry is the study of shapes.

_____ ❻ **Why does Wade's family meet with an architect?**

Ⓐ Architects notice shapes all around them.

Ⓑ The architect will help them design their new home.

Ⓒ Wade read about a famous house called "Fallingwater."

Ⓓ They want to move into a new apartment.

Word Power

Choose the English word from the Vocabulary list that correctly matches the definition.

 formed; made with

_____

 an area of math that deals with points, lines, shapes, etc.

_____

 a person who designs homes and buildings

_____

 the way something has been made or put together

_____

LESSON 17
Use of Language

Reading Tip

- Authors often use **figurative language** to describe ideas in a more vivid way. Figurative language includes **metaphors** and **similes**.

- Another way that authors use language to share a certain mood or image is through **dialogue** and the **voice of characters**. This passage has four characters (the narrator, the sister, the mom, and the dad).

Bad Hair Day

Skill Overview

Use of language refers to how an author uses words, expressions, and literary devices to help readers acquire meaning from a text. Examples include the use of **vivid verbs**, **strong adjectives**, **metaphor**, **point-of-view**, and **dialogue**.

When I woke up to the screeching of the alarm clock, I knew Melissa had tampered with the buttons. Instead of a Top 40 tune, I got scritch-scratch static as loud as a freight train in a tunnel. So after I picked my ears off the pillow and twisted them back into position, I shuffled like a **snail** into the hallway to wait my turn for the bathroom so that I could get ready for school.

Leaning against the wall like a newspaper on a doorstep was my **sinister** sister, smiling **mischievously**. Then she blurted out, "Your hair! You look like crows have made a **nest** on your head."

I lunged, my hands like vulture's claws pushing her to the ground. My dad barreled out of the bathroom, shaving cream covering his face. And when he shouted, "Get off your sister!" a big blob of shaving cream slithered into his mouth. The taste must have been awful, because right then he turned into a **chameleon**—turning pale green, yellow, and pink.

Then my dad looked at me and said, "Fix that mop, would you? Your hair looks like a tangle of thorns!"

I looked into the hall mirror, which stared back at me, silently **taunting**, "Nice hair! Hey, they might stick you in a zoo cage with hair like that!" I grabbed the hairbrush, but the thing seemed to tremble and bristle in terror as it neared my unruly mane. So I admitted defeat and sought assistance.

Feeling **dejected**, I padded into my mom's bedroom and pleaded for help. When she turned to look at me, her eyes twinkled, but her voice sympathized, "Another bad hair day?"

"Yes," I said, sitting on the edge of her bed as if waiting to get a shot at the doctor's.

Her slippers silently skittered under her bathrobe as she approached me, her hand holding a comb, with its sharp teeth glinting as if to say, "The more knots the better!" My hair was a **tangled** rope on a sailing vessel, and I dreaded every second of my mom's combing. I felt at least a billion hairs being yanked from my scalp, and I knew I'd soon be bald.

But when I finally looked in the mirror, I was transformed. I was a princess who had conquered the dragon—with a little help from the queen!

🎧 17

Vocabulary

snail
a small creature that has a soft, wet body and a round shell and moves very slowly

✪ **sinister**
evil; wicked

mischievously
in a way that displays slightly bad behavior but is not intended to cause serious harm or damage

nest
a structure built by birds or insects to leave their eggs in

✪ **chameleon**
an animal that can change colors to look like its surroundings

taunt
to intentionally annoy and upset someone

✪ **dejected**
extremely sad

tangled
twisted together in a knot

Reading Skill Comprehension Practice

Part 1

Describe what you noticed about the language in this passage.

The use of language is very descriptive / convincing / vivid . . .

_____

_____

_____

 **power up**

A **simile**

is a comparison that uses the word *like* or *as*.
"... static as loud as a freight train in a tunnel."

A **metaphor**

is a comparison that does not use these words.
"My hair was a tangled rope on a sailing vessel."

Part 2

List examples of metaphors and similes used in this passage.

1. My hair was a tangled rope on a sailing vessel.

2. _____
   _____

3. _____
   _____

4. _____
   _____

Part 3

Reread the passage, paying special attention to the dialogue. What does it tell you about the story? Write your ideas below.

_____

_____

_____

_____

Comprehension Review

Fill in the best answer for each question.

_____ ❶ *I got scritch-scratch static as loud as a freight train in a tunnel.*

What is this sentence an example of?

Ⓐ a simile   Ⓑ personification

Ⓒ a metaphor   Ⓓ dialogue

_____ ❷ **The narrator states that her dad** *turned into a chameleon—turning pale green, yellow, and pink.*

What does this really mean?

Ⓐ Her dad turned into an animal.

Ⓑ Her dad painted his face.

Ⓒ Her dad dressed up like an animal.

Ⓓ Her dad's face turned colors because of the awful taste in his mouth.

_____ ❸ *My hair was a tangled rope on a sailing vessel.*

In this _____ , the narrator compares her hair to a length of rope.

Ⓐ simile   Ⓑ metaphor

Ⓒ personification   Ⓓ poem

_____ ❹ **We can infer that this story takes place _____**

Ⓐ at dinnertime.

Ⓑ late at night.

Ⓒ in the morning.

Ⓓ at lunchtime.

_____ ❺ **Why did the narrator lunge at her sister, Melissa?**

Ⓐ Melissa made fun of her hair and tampered with the alarm clock.

Ⓑ Melissa woke her up too early.

Ⓒ Melissa combed her hair out and gave her a new hairstyle.

Ⓓ Melissa cut off all the narrator's hair.

_____ ❻ **At the end of the story, how does the narrator feel about her mother?**

Ⓐ angry

Ⓑ grateful

Ⓒ jealous

Ⓓ curious

Word Power

Choose the English word from the Vocabulary list that correctly matches the definition.

 evil; wicked

_____

 twisted together in a knot

_____

 extremely sad

_____

 an animal that can change colors to look like its surroundings

_____

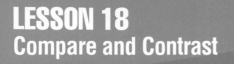
Deer

Biomes

Skill Overview

Authors use a compare-and-contrast structure to show similarities and differences between topics, events, or people. Readers may recognize this pattern by the use of certain signal words such as *like*, *but*, *also*, and *no*.

18

Different species of plants and animals live in different places called *biomes*. Each biome has different **conditions**: cold or hot, wet or dry. The conditions in each biome **determine** which plants and animals can live there.

Tundra and Taiga

At the extreme north of the world in the **tundra** biome, the weather is incredibly cold. Strong, cold winds sweep across the flat tundra. The top layer of soil freezes in winter and thaws in the summer; below that is a permanently frozen layer called *permafrost*. Permafrost keeps water from draining, creating ponds and bogs. Trees cannot grow in the tundra because their roots cannot get past the permafrost. Instead, tundra regions grow grasses, **lichens**, and mosses. Tundra animals include caribou, wolves, polar bears, and snowy owls.

Just south of the tundra is the largest land biome: taiga, which covers much of Canada, Russia, and China. Its devastating winters are long and cold,

Tundra

Snowy owl
Polar bear
Wolf
Caribou

Racoon

Fox

Rabbits

Squirrel

while its summers are brief and cool. The taiga has evergreen trees, which don't lose their leaves in winter. Animals that need trees can live in the taiga, too; birds nest in the trees, and deer hide in the shade.

Forests, Grasslands, and Deserts

South in the **temperate** forest, the warmer weather supports four seasons instead of just two. Some of the temperate forest's trees and **shrubs** are deciduous, meaning they lose their leaves annually. Maple, beech, and oak trees are common examples. The leaves gather sunlight during the spring and summer using photosynthesis. Each plant stores the energy for the winter, **discarding** its leaves when it doesn't need them. Deer, raccoons, foxes, rabbits, and squirrels make their homes in these forests.

The grassland is a biome found in areas with hot, dry summers and **mild**, wet winters. Every continent except Antarctica contains this biome. In Africa, zebras and giraffes graze on the grasslands. Buffalo once lived on the North American plains, which are grasslands. Grasslands have bushes that never grow over 10 feet tall.

The dry desert biome hardly ever gets rain because mountains block the winds that bring rain clouds. During the day, the Sun scorches the land, bringing the temperature to 50°C (122°F) in the shade! Then at night, the temperature drops close to freezing. Desert plants have adapted to these harsh conditions. Some have long water-seeking roots, whereas others, such as cacti, store water in their stems and roots.

Desert

Zebras

Giraffes

Buffalo

73

Reading Skill Comprehension Practice

 **Part 1** Think about why the author used a compare-and-contrast structure to describe biomes. Record your ideas below.

_____

_____

_____

 **Part 2** Choose two of the biomes described in the passage. Use the Venn diagram to compare and contrast them.

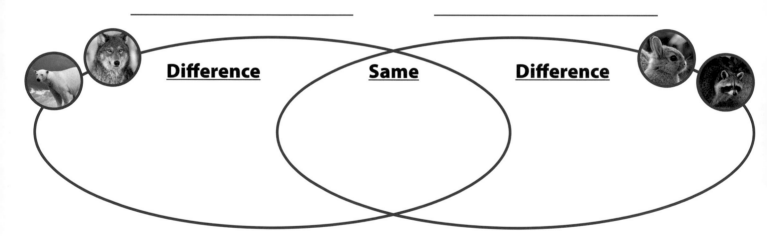

_____   _____

Difference   **Same**   **Difference**

Part 3 List other topics that would be appropriate for a compare-and-contrast text.

Other topics that would be appropriate for a compare-and-contrast text include

_____

_____

Comprehension Review

Fill in the best answer for each question.

_____ **1** Unlike the tundra, the taiga _____
- **A** has permafrost.
- **B** has animals.
- **C** can support trees.
- **D** is frozen all year.

_____ **2** What is one difference between Antarctica and the other continents?
- **A** Antarctica has no biomes.
- **B** Antarctica has a lot of rain.
- **C** Antarctica has many more animals.
- **D** Antarctica has no grasslands.

_____ **3** Forests, grasslands, and deserts are all _____
- **A** frozen.
- **B** biomes.
- **C** tropical.
- **D** dry climates.

_____ **4** Which biome is the farthest north?
- **A** tundra
- **B** grassland
- **C** taiga
- **D** desert

_____ **5** Grasslands, taiga, and tundra all have _____
- **A** permafrost.
- **B** four seasons.
- **C** animals.
- **D** trees.

_____ **6** Why does the temperate forest have four seasons instead of two?
- **A** The weather is too cold for two seasons.
- **B** The warmer weather supports four seasons.
- **C** There are trees in grasslands.
- **D** Most people live in this biome.

Word Power

Choose the English word from the Vocabulary list that correctly matches the definition.

plantlike organism

_____

having temperatures that are neither too cold nor too hot

_____

a large plant with a rounded shape formed from many small branches

_____

a cold, treeless area with permanently frozen subsoil

_____

Marc van Roosmalen: Fighter for Biodiversity

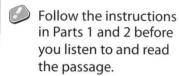

Reading Tip

- Follow the instructions in Parts 1 and 2 before you listen to and read the passage.

- This passage tells the story of a man who studies the plants and animals of the Amazon.

A pygmy marmoset

Skill Overview

A reader's prior knowledge includes information and experience that he or she has gained in the past. When readers are able to make connections between their prior knowledge and what they are reading, their comprehension is enhanced.

In 1997, an Indian from the Amazon Basin arrived at the Brazilian home of biologist Marc van Roosmalen. The Indian was holding a tin can with a little monkey inside. The Dutchman poked a finger at the small ball of fur. It squeaked with fear.

76

HERVE COLLART / CORBIS

Van Roosmalen nearly squeaked back—with surprise. He is an **expert** on **chimps** and apes. But he found himself staring at an unknown **species** of pygmy marmoset. It was an amazing **discovery**. The Indian knew only that the marmoset had been trapped somewhere near the Madeira River. This river flows into the Amazon. This clue sent van Roosmalen on a nine-month odyssey.

The Journey Begins

Van Roosmalen's quest led him into an unstudied region of the Amazon. The region is rich with **biodiversity**. So far, he and his team have discovered seven species of **primates**. They have also found a lost cousin of the Brazil nut tree and a plant with leaves bigger than elephant ears. And best of all, van Roosmalen found traces of an ancient farming technique. It had been invented by Stone Age tribes around 10,000 years ago.

Van Roosmalen also studies medicinal plants and rain forest **conservation**. In South America, he studied spider monkeys in their tree homes. Often, he survived on fruit gnawed by monkeys and then tossed away. "I was quite hungry," he recalls. "Spider monkeys are very economical eaters."

Spider Man

Inside the rain forest, van Roosmalen glides quietly through the foliage. Suddenly, raindrops shake off a tree high in the canopy. Van Roosmalen turns his **binoculars** upward. A branch bounces, and out pops a new species of monkey his team recently identified.

As the discoverer of the species, van Roosmalen has the right to choose its scientific name. But fame means less to him than saving a pure, green section of the Amazon. If not, he warns, "The rain forest will be destroyed before we even know what plants and animals are out there."

What Is Biodiversity?

Variety is the spice of life. This variety is what biodiversity is all about. Experts say there may be 3 million to 30 million different species of life on Earth. Some scientists believe that half of these species will become extinct by the year 2050. Habitats, or environments, can lose their biodiversity quickly. For example, when a single plant in a habitat vanishes, certain animals that need that plant to survive may also die out.

Vocabulary

expert
a person with a high level of knowledge or skill related to a particular subject or activity

chimp
abbreviation of *chimpanzee*, a small, very intelligent African ape with black or brown fur

species
a group of animals or plants of the same kind that can reproduce with each other

discovery
the process of finding information, a place, or an object

✪**biodiversity**
diversity among plant and animal species in an environment

✪**primate**
a member of the most developed and intelligent group of mammals, including humans, monkeys, and apes

conservation
the act of protecting natural resources such as plants and trees

binoculars
a pair of tubes with glass lenses at either end that are used to view faraway objects more clearly

Reading Skill Comprehension Practice

Part 1 Describe a time when you read or learned something new that helped you extend or adjust your existing knowledge about a topic.

_____

_____

_____

_____

_____

Part 2 Describe what you already know or think about biodiversity.

_____

_____

_____

_____

_____

Part 3 Now that you have read the passage about biodiversity, think about how your knowledge of this topic has changed. What about this text was surprising to you?

The part of the text that surprised me was _____

_____

_____

_____

_____

Comprehension Review

Fill in the best answer for each question.

❶ Using what you know about _____ makes it easier to understand this passage.

Ⓐ animals

Ⓑ spiders

Ⓒ math

Ⓓ rivers

❷ What is one thing this passage tells you about the Amazon rain forest?

Ⓐ Marc van Roosmalen is an expert on spiders

Ⓑ It is easy to protect the rainforest.

Ⓒ Several new species of primates have been discovered in the Amazon rain forest.

Ⓓ Monkeys cannot live in the rain forest.

❸ How does the sidebar help readers understand van Roosmalen's work?

Ⓐ It tells more about his work as a scientist.

Ⓑ It explains what biodiversity is and why it is importantin the rain forest.

Ⓒ It tells about his life.

Ⓓ It gives a synonym for the word *habitat*.

❹ Which is *not* an item van Roosmalen would likely take on a journey through the Amazon?

Ⓐ waterproof boots

Ⓑ binoculars

Ⓒ a wide-brimmed hat

Ⓓ a heavy coat

❺ What can we infer about Marc van Roosmalen?

Ⓐ He does not work hard.

Ⓑ He is not interested in learning.

Ⓒ He is curious.

Ⓓ He is ungrateful.

❻ If van Roosmalen had not journeyed through the Amazon, he would probably _____

Ⓐ have worked in a laboratory.

Ⓑ have failed to discover new plants and animal species.

Ⓒ told someone else to study the Amazon.

Ⓓ taken a monkey for a pet.

Word Power

Choose the English word from the Vocabulary list that correctly matches the definition.

1 diversity among plant and animal species in an environment

_____

2 the act of protecting natural resources like plants and trees

_____

3 a group of animals or plants of the same kind that can reproduce with each other

_____

4 a person with a high level of knowledge or skill related to a particular subject or activity

_____

Velociraptor

Skill Overview

A topic sentence introduces and summarizes the information to be covered in a paragraph. Effective readers use topic sentences to determine the main idea, locate information, and make predictions. This helps readers to better understand and interpret a text.

🎧 20

Velociraptor was a small **predatory** dinosaur. It lived about 75 million years ago. It was about seven feet long and weighed about 35 pounds. The name *Velociraptor* means "swift thief." Fossil evidence shows that this little dinosaur must have been a fast, effective **hunter**.

Its forearms were very thin and birdlike. It had long fingers with sharp claws, perfect for holding on to struggling **prey**. Long, slim legs would have given Velociraptor the speed to catch its food. Each foot had a huge claw on it that could have made large gashes in its victim. The "killing claws" on its feet were very large. In fact, the claws had to be held off the ground so Velociraptor could

walk and run. Scientists think that Velociraptor may have hunted in packs, like wolves do today. These creatures likely worked in groups to bring down larger prey.

Velociraptor's head was long. Its jaws were filled with small, sharp teeth. Its eyes were positioned to tilt slightly forward. This helped it gauge the distance to prey more accurately.

Velociraptor had a long, thin tail. Its tail was stiffened with a network of bony tendons. This tail helped it balance when running. The tail also may have helped it change direction quickly while **sprinting** after its supper.

Fossils of Velociraptor were found recently in Mongolia. These fossils tell us that Velociraptor had **feathers**. Feathers were good for keeping warm. They also helped signal or attract other velociraptors.

The "raptor" dinosaurs had many birdlike **adaptations**. Because of this, many **paleontologists** believe that modern-day birds are **descended from** Velociraptor and its relatives.

Velociraptor

Vocabulary

✪predatory
surviving by hunting and killing other animals

hunter
a person or an animal that chases wild animals for food

prey
an animal that is hunted by another animal for food

✪sprint
to run with great speed

feather
one of the many soft, light things that cover a bird's body

adaptation
the process of changing to suit different conditions

paleontologist
a scientist who studies fossils to learn about life long ago

descend from
to develop from something that existed in the past

Reading Skill Comprehension Practice

Part 1 Read the topic sentence from the passage below, and use it to predict what the passage will be about.

Topic Sentence

Velociraptor was a small predatory dinosaur.

My Prediction

Part 2 After reading **Velociraptor**, use the space below to describe what the passage is actually about.

What the Passage Is About

Part 3 This story's topic sentence is also its main idea: "Velociraptor was a small predatory dinosaur." Below is an example of a supporting detail from the passage. Add two more supporting details to the list.

Detail 1: Fossil evidence shows that this little dinosaur must have been a fast, effective hunter.

Detail 2:

Detail 3:

Comprehension Review

Fill in the best answer for each question.

_____ **❶ Which of these is the topic sentence of the first paragraph?**

Ⓐ The "raptor" dinosaurs had many birdlike adaptations.

Ⓑ Velociraptor had a long, thin tail.

Ⓒ Velociraptor was a small predatory dinosaur.

Ⓓ It lived about 75 million years ago.

_____ **❷ The topic sentence tells you that the main idea of this passage is _____**

Ⓐ what made Velociraptor a good hunter.

Ⓑ Velociraptor's large size.

Ⓒ that _Velociraptor_ means "swift thief."

Ⓓ that archaeologists have found Velociraptor bones in Mongolia, China, and southern Russia.

_____ **❸ Which of these is the topic sentence of the fifth paragraph?**

Ⓐ Velociraptor was a fierce predatory dinosaur.

Ⓑ Velociraptor was a meat eater with large claws and slim legs.

Ⓒ Fossils of Velociraptor were found recently in Mongolia.

Ⓓ Velociraptor was a fierce meat-eating dinosaur that lived about 75 million years ago.

_____ **❹ What was one effect of Velociraptor's long, slim legs?**

Ⓐ It could eat meat.

Ⓑ It was mean looking.

Ⓒ It had a slender tail.

Ⓓ It could run very fast.

_____ **❺ How do we know about Velociraptor?**

Ⓐ Archaeologists have found and studied its bones.

Ⓑ People can see it in zoos.

Ⓒ Ancient people saw it frequently and wrote about it.

Ⓓ Scientists have seen pictures of it.

_____ **❻ What might be a reason for Velociraptor's long, sharp claws?**

Ⓐ to hide from danger

Ⓑ to run very fast

Ⓒ to support its narrow head

Ⓓ to catch prey and win battles with other dinosaurs

Word Power

Choose the English word from the Vocabulary list that correctly matches the definition.

1 a scientist who studies fossils to learn about life long ago

_____

2 to run with great speed

_____

3 a person or animal that chases wild animals for food

_____

4 surviving by hunting and killing other animals

_____

Reading Tip

The author uses this story about a father and his three sons to teach you a lesson.

The Bundle of Sticks

Skill Overview

An author writes a text with a purpose in mind—often to persuade, inform, or entertain. Authors use specific devices to express the purpose. When readers are familiar with tools such as **word choice**, **persuasive techniques**, and **language structure**, they can more quickly determine the author's message.

There once lived a merchant who was the proud father of three fine sons. However, the sons never stopped **quarreling** with one another. The father often told them how much easier life would be if they would work together, but they paid absolutely no attention to his **advice**.

Finally, their **constant** fighting became more than the merchant could bear, so he **devised** a plan to show them that they needed to stick together. He called all his sons together and said, "My sons, the time is coming when I will no longer be with you. You will have to run the family business together and must learn to **rely on** each other. Yet, the way the three of you fight, I cannot imagine you working together productively. So do this for me: Gather a bundle of sticks, tie it with string, and bring it here."

When the sons returned with the bundle of sticks, the father said, "Take the bundle just as it is and break it in two. Whichever one of you can do that will **inherit** everything I own."

The eldest son tried first. He put his knee on the bundle and pressed and pulled with all his strength, but he could not bend the wood. Then the middle son and finally the youngest son tried, yet each failed. None of them could break the bundle.

"Father, you have given us an impossible task!" they cried. The merchant nodded, then reached for the bundle, undid the string, and removed three sticks, handing one to each son.

"Now try," he said. All three sons easily snapped their sticks across their knees.

Then the merchant asked, "Now do you understand what I mean? When you work together, you will be strong, and your business will **prosper**. But if you argue and go your **separate** ways, your enemies may break you."

Vocabulary

quarrel
to fight or argue

advice
an opinion

constant
happening a lot or all the time

devise
to invent or think of

rely on
to depend on someone or something; to have confidence in someone

inherit
to receive money, a house, etc., from someone after his or her death

prosper
to succeed at or make money doing something

separate
in different directions; independent

Reading Skill Comprehension Practice

Part 1 Why do you think the author uses an interesting story to teach the reader a lesson?

I think the author uses an interesting story to teach the reader a lesson because

Part 2 Identify the author's purpose for writing this passage. Then give the clues in the text that led you to this purpose.

Author's Purpose

Text Clues

Part 3 Describe the devices the author uses to express his or her message in this passage.

The devices the author uses include

Comprehension Review

Fill in the best answer for each question.

_____ **❶ Why did the author write this story?**

Ⓐ to explain what a merchant is

Ⓑ to teach a lesson

Ⓒ to complain about sons

Ⓓ to get readers to buy sticks

_____ **❷ Why did the merchant ask his sons to break the sticks?**

Ⓐ to show them how easy it is to break sticks

Ⓑ to show them how to compete

Ⓒ to show them how important it is to work together

Ⓓ to show them how to tie string

_____ **❸ The author hopes that _____**

Ⓐ readers will learn a lesson about working together.

Ⓑ readers will learn about fathers and sons.

Ⓒ readers will learn to break sticks.

Ⓓ readers will learn to gather bundles of sticks.

_____ **❹ After this lesson, the merchant's sons will probably _____**

Ⓐ fight even more.

Ⓑ get more sticks.

Ⓒ get angry with their father.

Ⓓ work together more often.

_____ **❺ The merchant was afraid that _____**

Ⓐ his sons would never learn to work as a team.

Ⓑ his youngest son would be jealous of the other sons.

Ⓒ his sons would not be able to find any sticks.

Ⓓ his sons would be lazy.

_____ **❻ In this story, what does the bundle of sticks represent?**

Ⓐ the merchant

Ⓑ the business

Ⓒ the merchant's sons

Ⓓ the fighting

Word Power

Choose the English word from the Vocabulary list that correctly matches the definition.

 to succeed at or make money doing something

_____

 to invent or think of

_____

 to receive money, a house, etc., from someone after his or her death

_____

 to fight or argue

_____

Reading Tip

In this lesson, you will learn about point of view in a story.

A New Grandfather

Skill Overview

Point of view refers to the specific perspective that is used in a piece of literature. Usually, the point of view is assigned to the narrator, or storyteller. The narrator may be a central character in the story (first-person point of view), or the narrator may tell a story about other people (third-person point of view).

We peeled ourselves out of the station wagon, the vinyl imprinted on the backs of our legs, and stretched. Finally, we were at my grandmother's new house, only minutes away from the amusement park!

"You're here to meet your new grandfather," our parents reminded us, as my brothers and I noticed the oranges in the trees lining the driveway, the lemons and limes in bushel baskets near the front door, and grapefruits dangling from the branches like softballs.

My grandmother met us at the front door, as did my new grandfather. As I waited my turn for hugs and kisses, I **analyzed** my new granddad. He didn't look new. He looked old, just like a granddad should. When he hugged me, he **tousled** my hair; his arms were strong, and he didn't want to let me go. Plus, he whispered, "I bet you can't wait to ride the **roller coaster**!" He knew the real reason we had driven for nearly three days.

I smiled. The only thing that felt new about my granddad was the house. I didn't know where we were to sleep or recognize the fancy chandelier over the dining room table. I had never seen the medals shining behind glass, the camel saddle, or the ivory statues hiding in the ferns. I didn't know about the brick path that led to a private backyard beach nor the boat docked in the lake.

But after several **visits**, the house became more and more **familiar** to me. Now I have many memories of my time there with my new grandfather. We would sit in the lake together, and Granddad would hold my tips up while I learned to water ski. Later, he would sit in the window while I slalomed around the lake. I remember him telling our favorite stories over and over—about Annapolis, the war, the Purple Heart.

My granddad was never really "new" to me. But he did give me new memories that I will **cherish** forever—memories of his house on the lake, the lemon trees, and yes, the roller coaster. Most of all, I remember my granddad's love and **generosity**. Because once upon a time, long, long ago, I was new to him. And he **treated** his new granddaughter as if we had always been together.

Vocabulary

analyze
to study or examine something in detail

tousle
to make messy, as in hair

roller coaster
an exciting ride in an amusement park

visit
an occasion when someone goes to see a place or person

familiar
easy to recognize because of being seen, met, heard, etc., before

cherish
to think of something as very special

generosity
the act of giving to others

treat
to behave toward someone or deal with something in a particular way

Reading Skill Comprehension Practice

 **power up**

A **first-person** narrative is a story narrated by one character who always refers to himself or herself in the first person, using words such as *I* and *we*.

A **third-person** narrative is a story told by a narrator who is separate from the characters of the story, using words such as *he*, *she*, and *they*.

 **Part 1** Identify the point of view of this passage. Then explain why you think the author chose this point of view. Did it help make the story more interesting?

The point of view of this passage is . . . I think the author chose

this point of view to . . .

_____

_____

_____

Part 2 Write a short story about yourself using a first-person point of view.

_____

_____

_____

Part 3 Rewrite your story from Part 2 using a third-person point of view.

_____

_____

_____

Comprehension Review

Fill in the best answer for each question.

❶ This story is told from _____ point of view.

Ⓐ Grandad's

Ⓑ Grandma's

Ⓒ the parents'

Ⓓ the grandaughter's

❷ How did the narrator's opinion of her grandfather change when she met him?

Ⓐ She recognized him.

Ⓑ She decided he seemed just like a granddad should.

Ⓒ She disliked him.

Ⓓ She discovered that he was not her grandfather.

❸ Why did the house seem new to the narrator?

Ⓐ She had not been there before.

Ⓑ The house had just been painted.

Ⓒ The house was just being built.

Ⓓ She was in the wrong house.

❹ Why did the narrator's opinion of the house change?

Ⓐ Her grandparents sold the house and moved.

Ⓑ She stopped visiting her grandparents.

Ⓒ She visited so often, the house became familiar.

Ⓓ She moved away.

❺ Where does this story probably take place?

Ⓐ near a mountain

Ⓑ near an amusement park

Ⓒ near a large city

Ⓓ near a cattle farm

❻ The narrator's grandfather probably _____

Ⓐ fought in a war.

Ⓑ was a cowboy.

Ⓒ was a farmer.

Ⓓ sang in a band.

Word Power

Choose the English word from the Vocabulary list that correctly matches the definition.

the act of giving to others

_____

to think of something as very special

_____

an occasion when someone goes to see a place or person

_____

make messy, as in hair

_____

Reading Tip

- Follow the instruction in Part 1 before you listen to and read the passage.

- This passage is a **business letter** addressed to the owner of a flower shop.

- Pay attention to the different parts of the business letter, including the sender's and the recipient's **addresses**, the **salutation**, the **body**, and the **closing**.

Skill Overview

When readers draw conclusions, they are analyzing information presented in the text against their own background knowledge. Authors often omit certain information because they assume readers will figure it out. Understanding information and interpreting it correctly is central to readers' ability to draw conclusions.

Nom de Plume
Research

23

"What's in a name? That which we call a rose by any other name would smell as sweet.,"

—Act II, Scene II Romeo and Juliet

987 Sweet Pea Drive
Fragrance, TN 45698

Freda's Flower Shop
564 Rose Lane
Tulip, TN 45682

September 15, 2008

Dear Madam:

Freda, after much **research**, I have found your name and its meaning. Your name **appropriately** means "peaceful." I say appropriately because the few times I've been in your shop, you have always been such a quiet and relaxed person. You make all those who are in your presence experience your **calming** nature. Your voice and **mannerisms** not only **reflect** your inner peace but allow those around you the **pleasure** of feeling safe and **unhurried** in a world that moves way too fast most of the time.

It has been a pleasure to research your name. I do not charge for my services because I am repaid in full by meeting and **corresponding** with so many nice people. Enjoy your name and its meaning.

Sincerely,

Elvina Floyd

Vocabulary

research
a detailed study of a subject

appropriately
suitably or correctly, given the situation or occasion

calming
peaceful, quiet, and without worry

✪**mannerism**
way of acting or behaving

reflect
to show

pleasure
enjoyment, happiness, or satisfaction

✪**unhurried**
not hurried, or leisurely and slow

correspond
to communicate in writing

Reading Skill Comprehension Practice

Draw some conclusions about this passage based on its format, and write them below.

_____

_____

_____

power up

- *Explicit* refers to information that is clearly stated in a text.
- *Implicit* refers to information that is understood but not directly stated.

Part **2** Record examples of both Explicit and Implicit information from the letter.

Explicit **Information**	Implicit **Information**
1. The person receiving the letter is Freda.	**1.** Freda works at a flower shop.
2.	**2.**

Part **3** Answer the questions below by drawing conclusions about the passage.

1. How does the sender feel about Freda? How do you know?

_____

_____

2. Why did the sender likely take the time to write this letter to a stranger?

_____

_____

3. What does the author want the reader to learn or understand?

_____

_____

4. What opinions have you formed about the sender based on explicit or implicit information in the letter?

_____

Comprehension Review

Fill in the best answer for each question.

_____ **❶ From this letter, we can infer that the sender has probably _____**

Ⓐ gone to the beach.

Ⓑ bought flowers.

Ⓒ gone on a cruise.

Ⓓ bought clothes at a mall.

_____ **❷ Fragrance, TN, and Tulip, TN, are probably _____**

Ⓐ very far apart.

Ⓑ fairly close together.

Ⓒ in different countries.

Ⓓ in the northern United States.

_____ **❸ How does Elvina Floyd feel about researching people's names?**

Ⓐ She really enjoys it.

Ⓑ She does not like it.

Ⓒ She is not good at it.

Ⓓ She is not used to it.

_____ **❹ _Your name appropriately means "peaceful."_ What is another word for _appropriately_?**

Ⓐ surprisingly

Ⓑ unfortunately

Ⓒ occasionally

Ⓓ fittingly

_____ **❺ Elvina thinks that Freda is _____**

Ⓐ unpleasant.

Ⓑ well named.

Ⓒ helpful.

Ⓓ loud.

_____ **❻ How did Freda likely hear of Elvina's services?**

Ⓐ She saw a newspaper ad.

Ⓑ She got a free coupon.

Ⓒ She met Elvina when Elvina came into her flower shop.

Ⓓ She delivered flowers to Elvina's office.

Word Power

Choose the English word from the Vocabulary list that correctly matches the definition.

 to communicate in writing

_____

 way of acting or behaving

_____

 not hurried, or leisurely and slow

_____

 to show

_____

Reading Tip

As you listen to and read the passage, think about the ideas proposed by the narrator and how he or she supports those ideas.

Author Envy

Skill Overview

A **proposition-and-support** pattern in text presents a proposition, theory, or problem and offers examples to support the theory or solve the problem. Successful readers identify patterns and use appropriate strategies to better understand a text.

🎧24

I really **admire** authors. They have a **talent** for being so **articulate**, an ability to affect people through words, and a capacity for **empathy**. Because writing is so much fun, I **envy** the author's job. Putting your feelings on a page is very difficult for some. Not everyone can open his or her heart by putting words on paper to share with the entire world. However, I feel fortunate that there are some people who find writing such an easy task!

admire
to find someone or something attractive and pleasant

talent
a natural ability to be good at something

articulate
clearly understandable

✪**empathy**
awareness of another person's feelings

envy
to want what someone else has

extraordinary
very unusual, special

reach
to touch or come to a place

quote
a phrase or short piece of writing

Authors create stories on a page, realizing and respecting the power of words. They know how words can manipulate, persuade, anger, or calm. They know that words can create laughter, cause people to weep, or take people to another world.

Authors are special people who take the risk of sharing a part of themselves with others. They write things that peer into my life, offer words of encouragement, or provide comfort. They may also chastise me or act as my conscience. Authors surely take joy in knowing that the words they write today will live on forever. I admire that, too. Authors are **extraordinary** people who **reach** into my heart and touch my soul. Sometimes, they also catch my attention with one small story or a **quote** that never lets me go.

Reading Skill Comprehension Practice

Part 1 Identify one of the propositions in this passage. Write it on the left side of the T-chart. Then identify the supports for this particular idea.

Proposition

_____

_____

_____

Supports

_____

_____

_____

Part 2 Choose one of the ideas below and circle it. Then write three reasons to support it.

Ⓐ It is everyone's job to clean up trash and keep the school clean.

Ⓑ Turning in homework on time is a student's responsibility.

Reason #1

_____

_____

_____

_____

_____

_____

Reason #2

_____

_____

_____

_____

_____

_____

Reason #3

_____

_____

_____

_____

_____

_____

Comprehension Review

Fill in the best answer for each question.

_____ ❶ *I really admire authors.*

Which statement does *not* support this proposition?

Ⓐ They make me feel envy.

Ⓑ They have a talent for being articulate.

Ⓒ They take the risk of sharing a part of themselves with others.

Ⓓ They realize and respect the power of words.

_____ ❷ *Because writing is so much fun.*

Which proposition does this support?

Ⓐ Authors create stories on a page.

Ⓑ Authors are special people.

Ⓒ I envy the author's job.

Ⓓ Not everyone can open his or her heart by putting words on paper to share with the entire world.

_____ ❸ **What is the main proposition in this passage?**

Ⓐ Authors write things that peer into my life and offer words of encouragement.

Ⓑ I really admire authors.

Ⓒ Authors surely take joy in knowing the words they write today will live on forever.

Ⓓ Putting your feelings on a page is very difficult for some.

_____ ❹ *They may also chastise me or act as my conscience.*

What does _chastise_ mean in this sentence?

Ⓐ praise

Ⓑ sing to

Ⓒ remind

Ⓓ scold

_____ ❺ **Which of these is *not* an opinion?**

Ⓐ They have a talent to be so articulate, an ability to affect people through words, and a capacity for empathy.

Ⓑ They know how words can manipulate, persuade, anger, or calm.

Ⓒ Authors create stories on a page.

Ⓓ Authors are special people.

_____ ❻ **Which sentence correctly states the narrator's opinion?**

Ⓐ Writing is fun.

Ⓑ Authors should be pitied.

Ⓒ Words are not powerful.

Ⓓ What authors do is not important.

Word Power

Choose the English word from the Vocabulary list that correctly matches the definition.

 1 awareness of another person's feelings

_____

 2 clearly understandable

_____

 3 to want what someone else has

_____

 4 to touch or come to a place

_____

LESSON 25
Graphic Features

Reading Tip

You can use graphic features to **determine main ideas, locate information**, and **make predictions**.

Upside Down

Skill Overview

Graphic features include visuals—such as **illustrations**, **photos**, **diagrams**, **maps**, **tables**, and **charts**—that add meaning to a text. These features help readers get more information from the written page. Often, a graphic feature can explain information in a more interesting and colorful way than simple text can.

retina

lens

pupil

cornea

iris

100

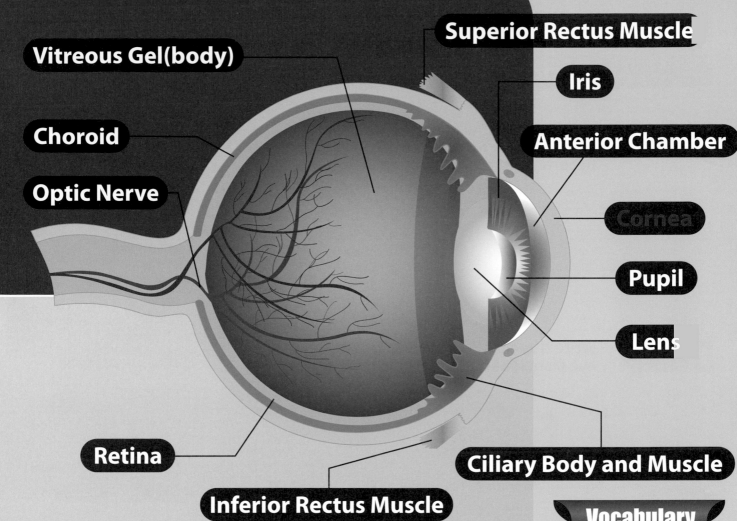

Vitreous Gel(body)

Superior Rectus Muscle

Iris

Choroid

Anterior Chamber

Optic Nerve

Cornea

Pupil

Lens

Retina

Ciliary Body and Muscle

Inferior Rectus Muscle

 25

Your eyes see things upside down. After light **enters** the **pupil**, it hits the lens, which is **located** behind the **iris**. The lens has the important job of focusing light rays on the back of the eyeball. The back of the eyeball is called the *retina*. The **retina** acts like a movie screen, but the "movie" in your eyes is upside down. Light passes through the lens and hits the retina, which **transmits** a message to the brain. The message that the brain **receives** is upside down. But the brain is very smart: It turns the image over so it is right-side up.

Did you know that your eyes see things upside down? It's true! The image is seen upside down, but the brain flips it around so you see it right-side up. Amazing!

Reading Skill Comprehension Practice

Part 1 Think about how graphic features can be used. How might they help a reader? Record your ideas below.

_____

_____

_____

_____

Part 2 Write three facts you learned about the eye from looking at the graphic features.

Fact 1
_____
_____

Fact 2
_____
_____

Fact 3
_____
_____

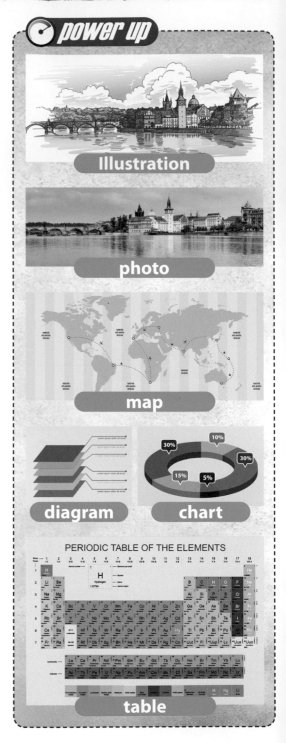

power up

Illustration

photo

map

diagram   chart

PERIODIC TABLE OF THE ELEMENTS

table

Part 3 Explain how the graphics showing the parts of the eye helped you understand the passage. Cite specific examples.

The graphic features helped me
_____
_____

Comprehension Review

Fill in the best answer for each question.

_____ **1** **Light enters your eye through the _____**

- Ⓐ retina.
- Ⓑ pupil.
- Ⓒ lens.
- Ⓓ brain.

_____ **2** **The lens focuses light on your _____**

- Ⓐ pupil.
- Ⓑ iris.
- Ⓒ retina.
- Ⓓ lens.

_____ **3** **The retina sends images to the _____, which flips them right-side up.**

- Ⓐ brain
- Ⓑ pupil
- Ⓒ lens
- Ⓓ iris

_____ **4** **Which happens _first_?**

- Ⓐ The brain turns images right-side up.
- Ⓑ Light is focused on the retina.
- Ⓒ Light enters the eye through the pupil.
- Ⓓ The retina sends images to the brain.

_____ **5** **_Light passes through the lens and hits the retina, which transmits a message to the brain._**

What does _transmits_ mean in this sentence?

- Ⓐ runs
- Ⓑ calls
- Ⓒ keeps
- Ⓓ sends

_____ **6** **Why is the retina compared to a movie screen?**

- Ⓐ We see movie screens best when it is dark.
- Ⓑ Images are focused on the retina, just as they are focused on a movie screen.
- Ⓒ The retina focuses light on the iris, just as a movie camera focuses light.
- Ⓓ Movie screens show images upside down.

Word Power

Choose the English word from the Vocabulary list that correctly matches the definition.

 1
the colored part around the pupil of the eye

_____

 2
the light-sensitive nerve membrane lining the back of the eye

_____

 3
the transparent part of the coat of the eyeball

_____

 4
the circular black area in the center of the eye

_____

Seal from the flag of Mexico showing the Aztec prophecy

City of the Aztecs

Reading Tip

- Follow the instruction in Part 1 before you listen to and read the passage.

- **Mental images** can come from your prior knowledge or from your experiences.

Skill Overview

Creating mental images when reading can help readers immerse themselves in a text. These mental images can be used to **draw conclusions**, **make inferences**, **fill in missing information**, and **recall important details**.

Hundreds of years ago, a group of ancient Aztecs decided to find a new home. They did not know where they were going, but their sun god had promised to help them find land. He said they should live where they saw an eagle sitting on a **cactus** and eating a snake. They found this place in central Mexico.

The Aztecs named their new city Tenochtitlan. It was located on an island in the middle of a lake. As it turned out, this location was perfect. They farmed the land by creating floating gardens in the **marshland**. These gardens were constructed by grouping **twigs** together and then adding mud on top. Plant roots often grew into the ground under the water. Among the Aztecs' crops were corn, beans, chilies, and tomatoes.

To get around the city, the Aztecs used **canoes** and built **canals**. In addition, they built highways leading across the lake to the mainland. If war threatened, they simply removed these highways, making it impossible for their enemies to reach them unless they had boats. In just a few years, the Aztecs built palaces, temples, ball courts, and even a zoo.

The Aztecs became one of the most powerful **empires** of the time. They were expert **warriors** and knew how to win in battle. They seemed **invincible**—until 1519, when the Spanish explorers arrived. Initially, the Aztecs believed the Spaniards were gods. But the Spanish, well-trained soldiers armed with guns, defeated the Aztecs and took over their city

THE GRANGER COLLECTION

Vocabulary

cactus
a desert plant that often has sharp spines and thick stems for storing water

marshland
an area of land that is soft and wet

twig
a small, thin branch of a tree or bush

canoe
a small, light, narrow boat that is pointed at both ends

canal
a long, thin stretch of water that is created for boats to travel along

empire
a group of countries that are all controlled by one ruler or government

warrior
a soldier

✪invincible
incapable of being defeated

Reading Skill Comprehension Practice

Part 1 Look at the pictures in the passage. What do these pictures make you think of? Write your ideas below.

_____

_____

Part 2 Think about the passage and answer the questions below.

What did you see?	What did you hear?	What did you smell?	What did you feel?
_____	_____	_____	_____
_____	_____	_____	_____
_____	_____	_____	_____
_____	_____	_____	_____

Part 3 Use your mental images to answer the following questions. You will be filling in missing information and making inferences based on what the author included in the text.

1. Why did the Aztecs decide to settle at the site that became Tenochtitlan?

_____

2. Why was the location perfect?

_____

3. How did the Aztecs grow their food?

_____

4. How would you describe the Aztec people?

_____

Comprehension Review

Fill in the best answer for each question.

____ ❶ Which mental picture would best help you understand the site where Tenochtitlan was built?

Ⓐ a map of Spain
Ⓑ an eagle on a cactus
Ⓒ an island in the middle of a lake
Ⓓ floating gardens

____ ❷ A picture of _____ would help you understand the words *floating gardens*.

Ⓐ flowers floating in water
Ⓑ groups of twigs with mud on top
Ⓒ gardens built on a boat
Ⓓ flowers floating in the air

____ ❸ Based on the passage, how should you picture the Aztecs protecting themselves from enemies?

Ⓐ by imagining the Aztecs shooting cannons
Ⓑ by imagining their enemies swimming across the lake
Ⓒ by imagining the Aztecs creating floating gardens
Ⓓ by imagining the Aztecs removing the highways to the mainland

____ ❹ What can the reader infer about the Aztecs' religious beliefs?

Ⓐ They respected and listened to their gods.
Ⓑ They thought the Spaniards were gods.
Ⓒ The sun god told them where they should live.
Ⓓ They did not have gods.

____ ❺ The author writes that the Aztecs seemed invincible. What does *invincible* mean in this passage?

Ⓐ incredible
Ⓑ unbelievable
Ⓒ unable to be defeated
Ⓓ able to be convinced

____ ❻ Why did the Aztecs likely think the Spaniards were gods?

Ⓐ The Spanish explorers arrived in 1519.
Ⓑ The Spaniards looked different from them.
Ⓒ The Spanish explorers spoke their language.
Ⓓ The Spaniards had been to the city before.

Word Power

Choose the English word from the Vocabulary list that correctly matches the definition.

 1 incapable of being defeated

_____

 2 a group of countries that are all controlled by one ruler or government

_____

 3 an area of land that is soft and wet

_____

 4 a long, thin stretch of water that is created for boats to travel along

_____

Chapter 2

Diseases

Germs All Around Us

- Follow the instruction in Part 1 before you listen to and read the passage.

- **Chapter titles** of both fiction and nonfiction books provide you with a great deal of information as you read.

- This chapter is from a book about diseases.

Skill Overview

Chapter titles can provide readers with valuable information and help them understand and interpret text. Readers can use chapter titles to **determine the main idea**, **locate information**, or **make predictions**.

Vocabulary

bacteria

fungi

protozoa

viruses

Theme

We live in a world filled with microbes—microscopic creatures such as **viruses**, **bacteria**, and **fungi**. A spoonful of dirt contains billions of them. And from your head to your toes, inside and out, you are home to trillions more of them. Most are harmless. Many are good—they help us digest our food, for example. But some can make us sick. We call these bad ones *germs*, or bugs.

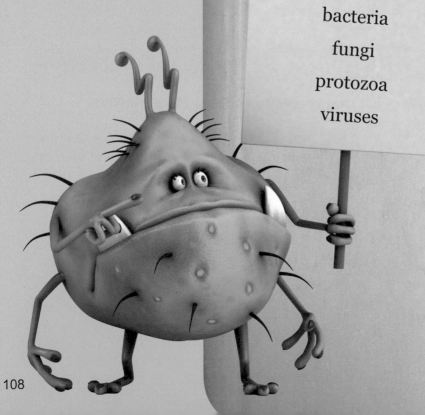

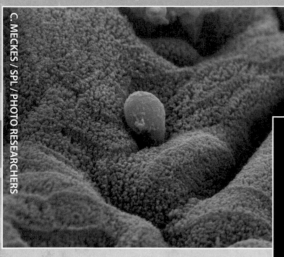

C. MECKES / SPL / PHOTO RESEARCHERS

◀ **This protozoon, the entamoeba, hangs out in foul water and the human gut. It causes bellyaches and diarrhea.**

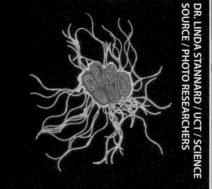

DR. LINDA STANNARD / UCT / SCIENCE SOURCE / PHOTO RESEARCHERS

▶ *Salmonella* **is a bacterium that can give you food poisoning or deadly typhoid fever.**

Vocabulary

virus
small living thing that can cause infectious illnesses

bacteria
small living things that sometimes cause disease

✪**fungi**
growing things similar to plants without leaves, usually found in wet places

germ
a very small organism that causes disease

resistance
the act of fighting against something that is attacking you

propel
to push or move something somewhere

immune
protected against a particular disease by particular substances in the blood

infection
a disease in a part of the body that is caused by bacteria or a virus

Sneak Attack

Germs can enter our bodies through the nose, mouth, or other openings. They may also enter through a cut in the skin. But if germs are all around us, why aren't we always sick?

Most of the time, our bodies fight off germs. But if we haven't been getting enough sleep or eating right, our **resistance**—the ability to fight off illness—slips. Then it becomes easier for germs to mount a sneak attack.

How Germs Spread

A single sneeze can **propel** millions of germs into the air. Hands that cover a cough still deposit germs on desks, doorknobs, and computer keyboards. Diseases spread in many other ways. We can become ill from germs in food that hasn't been handled or cooked properly. Water can also be contaminated with germs—such as protozoa—especially in poor countries.

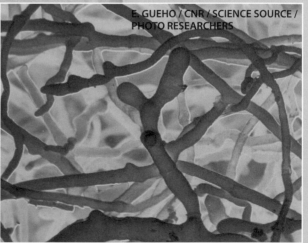

E. GUEHO / CNR / SCIENCE SOURCE / PHOTO RESEARCHERS

Trichophyton, **a.k.a. ringworm, is a fungus that lives on—and eats—your skin.**

Target: Children

Kids, especially little kids, get sick more often than grownups do. One reason is that their bodies have not yet mastered the art of recognizing and battling common germs. The cells of the **immune** system have the job of fighting germs. As we get older, these "soldiers" get better at fighting **infection**. This helps us become immune to many of the germs that made us sick as children

Reading Skill Comprehension Practice

 **Part 1** Complete the "Before Reading" box before listening to and reading the passage. Then take notes about the topic while listening to and reading the passage. Finally, finish the chart after listening to and reading the passage.

Before Reading

What questions or predictions do you have based on the title?

_____

_____

_____

During Reading

Take notes about the topic.

_____

_____

_____

After Reading

What did you learn?

_____

_____

_____

Further Research

What do you still want to know?

_____

_____

_____

 **Part 2** Think about the chapter title **Chapter 2: Diseases Germs All Around Us**. What do you think the main idea of this passage is? Write it below.

The main idea of this chapter is _____

_____

Part 3 The chapter title **Chapter 2: Diseases Germs All Around Us** helps a reader know what the chapter might be about. Think of other chapter titles that might help send the same message to the reader. Write your ideas

Germs Everywhere!

Comprehension Review

Fill in the best answer for each question.

_____ ❶ The subtitle "Germs All Around Us" tells you that this passage is mainly about _____
Ⓐ how germs cause illness.
Ⓑ bacteria.
Ⓒ the immune system.
Ⓓ fungi.

_____ ❷ "Chapter 2: Diseases" is another meaning clue. It tells you that this passage is about _____
Ⓐ fighting infections.
Ⓑ a deadly virus.
Ⓒ how diseases are spread.
Ⓓ food poisoning.

_____ ❸ What might be another good title for this chapter?
Ⓐ Germs in Our Food
Ⓑ Curing the Common Cold
Ⓒ The Immune System
Ⓓ Flu Season

_____ ❹ Which is *not* a way that germs enter our bodies?
Ⓐ nose
Ⓑ skin
Ⓒ mouth
Ⓓ hair

_____ ❺ Why do children get sick more often than grownups?
Ⓐ They have more germs.
Ⓑ They play outside more often.
Ⓒ Their bodies aren't as good at battling germs.
Ⓓ They don't know how to blow their noses.

_____ ❻ Which is *not* a microbe that causes illness?
Ⓐ antibody
Ⓑ virus
Ⓒ bacterium
Ⓓ fungus

Word Power

Choose the English word from the Vocabulary list that correctly matches the definition.

 1 growing things similar to plants without leaves, usually found in wet places
_____

 2 small living thing that can cause infectious illnesses
_____

 3 small living things that sometimes cause disease
_____

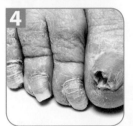 4 a disease in a part of the body that is caused by bacteria or a virus
_____

Ancient China

Reading Tip

This passage describes the various dynasties that ruled China. Pay close attention to **how the author organized** the passage as you listen to and read it.

Skill Overview

Authors structure texts in different ways to easily convey information to readers. Text that is written in chronological order tells the time order in which a process or series of events occurred. Developing an awareness of this text structure helps a reader to better understand a text.

🎧 28

The first Chinese settled in the Yellow River Valley. They were farmers and craftsmen. In addition to planting crops, they made pottery and silk. The first society was the Xia 夏 (she-AH) **Dynasty**. A dynasty is one family that holds the power in a nation over a period of time. The Xia ruled from about 2000 B.C. to 1600 B.C. The mountains along China's border kept it separate from other nations, so there was not a lot of trade during this time.

The Shang Dynasty 商

The Shang Dynasty held power from about 1600 B.C. to 1046 B.C. Its people used **bronze** to make tools and wheels. The oldest Chinese writings come from this time. The people carved words on animal shells and bones. These are called *oracle bones*.

The Great Wall of China

Long-Lasting Zhou Dynasty

Next, the Zhou (JO) Dynasty **reigned** for 900 years. This dynasty kept written records of what happened on a daily basis. The final Zhou **emperors** were weak and could not control the people. Many small states broke away. The armies of these states fought one another. Soon, civil war erupted. Thousands of men died in bloody battles. The countryside was destroyed.

Short But Sweet: the Qin Dynasty

The Qin (CHIN) Dynasty came after the fall of the Zhou. It lasted only about 15 years. Yet Emperor Qin Shi Huang (CHIN SHE HWANG) accomplished much in this short time. He ended the constant battles and **unified** the nation, taking control of all of China. Over the years, other leaders had built walls to protect their **territories**. Qin decided to join these walls and make them longer. This was the start of what became the Great Wall of China.

The Han Dynasty

When Qin died, his sons lost control of the country. The Han (HAWN) Dynasty began. Lasting more than 400 years, it was one of the strongest in Chinese history. During this time, China had a population of 60 million people, which made it the world's largest country. The Silk Road, a trade route from China to Europe, was finished during this time. It was the first link between Asia and European nations.

Once the Han dynasty **crumbled**, a period of wars followed. Barbarians **controlled** the northern part of China. Different rulers controlled parts of southern China.

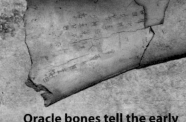

Oracle bones tell the early history of China

The Silk Road

113

Reading Skill Comprehension Practice

Compare and Contrast	Cause and Effect	Proposition and Support
───⟨≫⟩───	───⟨≫⟩───	───⟨≫⟩───
This structure shows similarities and differences.	This structure explains the result of an event or occurrence and the reasons it happened.	This structure presents a proposition, theory, or problem and offers details to support the theory or solve the problem.

 **Part 1** Think about how this passage is organized. Write your ideas below.

_____

_____

_____

 **Part 2** Passages can be organized in several different ways. Given the topic of this passage, which structure would be most effective? Write your ideas below.

The type of structure that makes the most sense for this passage is

_____

_____

Part 3 Answer the questions below about the passage.

1. How many Chinese dynasties are described in this passage?

2. Which dynasty was the **shortest**? Which was the **longest**? Which was the **strongest**?

3. Why was the Great Wall of China built?

4. What was the purpose of the Silk Road?

114

Comprehension Review

Fill in the best answer for each question.

_____ **❶ The Shang Dynasty reigned** _after_
_____

Ⓐ the Qin Dynasty.
Ⓑ the Zhou Dynasty.
Ⓒ the Xia Dynasty.
Ⓓ the Han Dynasty.

_____ **❷ Which dynasty came** _first_**?**

Ⓐ the Zhou Dynasty
Ⓑ the Xia Dynasty
Ⓒ the Qin Dynasty
Ⓓ the Han Dynasty

_____ **❸ When did Emperor Qin Shi Huang join the walls that eventually became the Great Wall of China?**

Ⓐ after the Silk Road was finished
Ⓑ after the Han dynasty began
Ⓒ before he took control of China
Ⓓ after he ended the battles to unify the nation

_____ **❹ According to the passage, which word does** _not_ **describe the dynasties?**

Ⓐ weary
Ⓑ powerful
Ⓒ mighty
Ⓓ unified

_____ **❺ Why wasn't there a lot of trade in China during the Xia dynasty?**

Ⓐ The Chinese did not trade during this time.
Ⓑ China had poor relations with nearby nations.
Ⓒ Mountains along China's border kept it separate.
Ⓓ It was not the best way to conduct business.

_____ **❻ Why was the Silk Road important?**

Ⓐ It was the primary trade route for the Xia Dynasty.
Ⓑ It was the first link between Asia and Europe.
Ⓒ It increased China's population.
Ⓓ It contributed to the period of wars after the Han Dynasty.

Word Power

Choose the English word from the Vocabulary list that correctly matches the definition.

the supreme ruler of an empire

_____

the land that is owned or controlled by a particular country

_____

to hold power or to rule

_____

a series of rulers from the same family or group

_____

LESSON 29
Fact and Opinion

Reading Tip

Both nonfiction and fiction texts may contain facts and opinions.

Skill Overview

Facts are true statements, while opinions reflect one's feelings or emotions. Both fiction and nonfiction texts may include both facts and opinions. Readers must be able to distinguish between fact and opinion in order to read a text critically and understand the author's message.

If an Atom in My Lunchroom Could Talk

I heard some whisperings as I walked past the lunchroom wall, so I put my ear closer. I knew I must be **delusional**, but it seemed real enough. This one **atom** in the wall was whispering its shared secrets of years past. What an opportunity for me! The president of the United States had attended this school 40 years ago. I might find out some interesting information about our country's leader.

What was that? My gym teacher had been a student at this very school with the president. He had thrown food, and did he get into trouble! What a character he was! This atom on the wall had seen and heard it all. This could prove to be an interesting day.

The **duration** of lunch was only 20 minutes, but I wanted to make the most of it. I pulled up a chair, sat down, and listened **intently** to information about events that occurred in this room. I quietly asked questions and **received** answers. Armed with information about the school, the administration, **faculty** members, and the president—I couldn't wait to spread some **gossip**.

Suddenly, Mr. Kim, my gym teacher, placed his hand on my shoulder. As he leaned over, he quietly commented about how I had found his secret source of information and warned me not to discuss talking walls. He promised that he wouldn't tell anyone that I thought walls talked if I didn't share the secrets that I now knew.

Lunch was over, and I hurried out of the cafeteria doors on my way to class. I **overheard** Mr. Kim whisper to me, "Talking walls—don't forget." Somehow I knew that he was talking from personal experience. There was no doubt in my mind; I would keep all of these secrets to myself forever.

117

Reading Skill Comprehension Practice

Part 1 Find a fact and an opinion from the passage and write them below.

Fact	Opinion
1. Lunch lasts 20 minutes.	**1.** This could prove to be an interesting day.
2.	**2.**

Part 2 Fill in the chart below with facts and opinions about four different topics.

BANANAS

Fact

Opinion

ROCK AND ROLL

Fact

Opinion

BICYCLES

Fact

Opinion

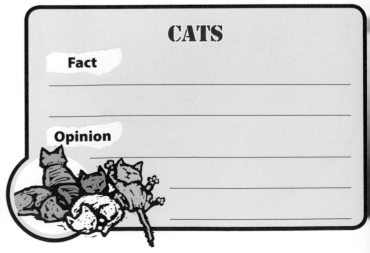

CATS

Fact

Opinion

Comprehension Review

Fill in the best answer for each question.

_____ **❶ The narrator's opinion is that** _____
- Ⓐ it could prove to be an interesting day.
- Ⓑ the duration of lunch was 20 minutes.
- Ⓒ Mr. Kim whispered, "Talking walls—don't forget."
- Ⓓ the gym teacher had been a student at the school.

_____ **❷ Which sentence is a fact?**
- Ⓐ What a character he was!
- Ⓑ This could prove to be an interesting day.
- Ⓒ Lunch was only 20 minutes.
- Ⓓ It seemed real enough.

_____ **❸ Which sentence tells you what the narrator thinks?**
- Ⓐ Suddenly, Mr. Kim, my gym teacher, placed his hand on my shoulder.
- Ⓑ What an opportunity for me!
- Ⓒ I pulled up a chair, sat down, and listened intently to information about events in this room.
- Ⓓ He had been throwing food, and did he get into trouble!

_____ **❹ Mr. Kim probably** _____
- Ⓐ is a math teacher.
- Ⓑ did not know the narrator was listening to a wall.
- Ⓒ knows a lot of secrets and gossip.
- Ⓓ never got into trouble at school.

_____ **❺ What can we infer?**
- Ⓐ Mr. Kim is about the same age as the author.
- Ⓑ Mr. Kim has never heard talking walls.
- Ⓒ Mr. Kim attended the school 40 years ago.
- Ⓓ The narrator knows nothing about Mr. Kim.

_____ **❻ How did the narrator find out about Mr. Kim throwing food?**
- Ⓐ The president told him.
- Ⓑ An atom on the wall told him.
- Ⓒ Mr. Kim told him.
- Ⓓ He read about it.

Word Power

Choose the English word from the Vocabulary list that correctly matches the definition.

with great concentration

_____

mistaken or tricked

_____

a length of time

_____

to hear what other people are saying without intending to

_____

THE TEST

Reading Tip

- Follow the instruction in Part 1 before you listen to and read the passage.

- This is a passage about a girl who is taking an important test in class.

- Readers should ask themselves two kinds of questions: **thought-provoking question** and **clarifying question**.

Skill Overview

Good readers ask questions before, during, and after reading. When readers are thinking of questions as they read, they are monitoring their own comprehension and reading for a particular purpose. Distinguishing between different kinds of questions is an important part of this strategy.

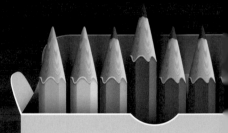

Lola yawned and stretched her arms high over her head. Three sharp cracks from Lola's spine **resounded** in the silent classroom, and several students giggled. Mr. Kojima's eyes **glared** around the room; then he placed a test on Kiley's desk. Kiley breathed and flipped through the pages, five in all. Mr. Kojima paced the aisles as the class scribbled, the steady click-click of his worn loafers keeping time with the clock. Kiley **glanced** at the clock over the doorway. Thirty minutes left.

Kiley tugged nervously at her long braids and stretched her head from side to side, first with eyes closed, then with eyes open. And that is when she saw it. There, in Lola's curled left hand was a piece of paper. As Mr. Kojima's clicks approached, Lola's left hand stealthily slithered under the desk. As he walked away, the hand returned and uncoiled the answers to the test.

Kiley pulled her chair closer to her desk, and the **screech** sent chills up her spine, as well as those of her classmates. Kiley **responded** to every question, remembering the study sessions with her mother, the after-school help with Mr. Kojima, the reading and rereading of notes, and the memorizing of facts—in place of trips to the mall, a baseball game, and the movies.

Some of the answers Kiley knew, and some she could only try her best to answer.

Lola finished first, and every class member watched her **march** to the front and flip the test onto Mr. Kojima's desk. Even Mr. Kojima looked surprised.

As Lola eased into her seat, she combed her shoulder-length blonde hair with her fingers and drummed her pretty, pink-polished fingernails on the desk.

The bell marking the end of class sounded more like a majorette's whistle signaling the band to begin. Kiley placed her test on the pile in Mr. Kojima's hands. She had finished but had no time to **review** her answers.

Kiley's eyes connected with several of her classmates. She felt a mixture of **relief** that the test was over and sadness that it was, indeed, over.

Kiley didn't know if she could stand seeing Lola, but she shared lockers with her, and memories, too. Could she be friends with a cheater?

Vocabulary

⚙ **resound**
to echo

glare
to look directly at someone or something in an angry way

glance
to give a quick, short look

⚙ **screech**
a sharp, high-pitched sound

respond
to say or do something as a reaction to something

⚙ **march**
to walk somewhere quickly and in a determined way

review
to consider something in order to make changes to it

relief
a feeling of happiness that something unpleasant has ended

Reading Skill Comprehension Practice

power up   Larger, **thought-provoking** questions help you analyze a text.
            ~~Smaller, clarifying~~ questions help you understand a text.

Part 1 Record three questions you have about the passage based on the title and the topic.

1. *Why does the girl need to take the test?*
2. _____
3. _____
4. _____

Part 2 Think of two additional questions you have about the passage.

Large Question

_____

_____

Small Question

_____

_____

Part 3 Reread Lesson 9, **Hydroponics**, and fill in the information below.

A **fact** about the topic:

_____

Question for a Friend

_____

_____

Question for the Author

_____

_____

Comprehension Review

Fill in the best answer for each question.

_____ ❶ **Which question is *not* answered in the passage?**

Ⓐ Who had the answers to the test?

Ⓑ How did Kiley prepare for the test?

Ⓒ Who finished the test first?

Ⓓ What subject does Mr. Kojima teach?

_____ ❷ **How was Lola able to cheat on the test?**

Ⓐ Lola had the answers.

Ⓑ Kiley gave her the answers.

Ⓒ Mr. Kojima told everyone the answers.

Ⓓ Kiley's mother helped Lola with the test.

_____ ❸ **Which question is *not* answered in the passage?**

Ⓐ What color is Lola's nail polish?

Ⓑ Who is the teacher?

Ⓒ Will Kiley tell Mr. Kojima what she saw?

Ⓓ Who does Kiley share her locker with?

_____ ❹ **This test was probably _____ for Kiley.**

Ⓐ too easy

Ⓑ a little hard

Ⓒ too hard

Ⓓ the very first test

_____ ❺ **Why did Lola finish her test so quickly?**

Ⓐ She had the test answers.

Ⓑ She studied more than Kiley did.

Ⓒ Mr. Kojima excused her from finishing the test.

Ⓓ The test was too easy for her.

_____ ❻ **What can we conclude?**

Ⓐ Nobody in the class knew that Lola had the test answers.

Ⓑ This was a math test.

Ⓒ Several students realized that Lola had cheated on the test.

Ⓓ Kiley's mother did not want her to do well on the test.

Word Power

Choose the English word from the Vocabulary list that correctly matches the definition.

 a sharp, high-pitched sound

_____

 to say or do something as a reaction to something

_____

 to consider something in order to make changes to it

_____

 to echo

_____

Review Test

Questions 1–15: Read the passage and answer the questions. Fill in the letter next to the answer choice you think is correct.

The Long Road West

Summary: Many Americans emigrated west to start a new life.

An artist depicts a scene from the trip along the Oregon Trail.

Background: By 1820, the population of the states and territories had doubled. People began to look west to live. Getting there was easier than ever, thanks to newly built canals, roads, and railroads. But there was one western region that was still difficult to reach: the Oregon Territory. This huge area was made up of what is now Oregon, Washington, Idaho, and British Columbia.

The Pioneers

The easiest way to reach Oregon was also the slowest: by ship around South America, which could take a year. The most direct path was over land, across the Great Plains: Oklahoma, Kansas, Nebraska, the Dakotas, Montana, and parts of Wyoming and Colorado. The only Americans who knew their way around Plains country were mountain men—fur traders who lived off the land. One of these mountain men, Jedidiah Smith, led the first expedition to the Oregon Territory. In 1832, he guided Nathaniel J. Wyeth and 24 other men west from St. Louis, Missouri. Smith took the men through a gap in the Rocky Mountains, called South Pass, and into Oregon.

In 1834, Wyeth made another trip to Oregon that changed history. People on this expedition spread the news back east about the wonders of Oregon. People heard tales about a region of great natural beauty, with endless supplies of wood, water, and fish. It created "Oregon Fever."

The Oregon Trail

The path to Oregon was called the Oregon Trail. From 1843 to 1868, about a half million people took this path to Oregon, as well as to Utah and California. Most men, women, and children left from Missouri on covered wagon trains. Sometimes 100 wagons, pulled by oxen or mules, made up this fleet. The trip was hard. Some settlers drowned or lost their belongings in dangerous streams and rivers. Others died from lightning and wagon accidents, or ran out of food and water. Sometimes (but not often) hostile American Indians were a threat. The worst danger on the trip was cholera, a deadly disease that spreads through bad sanitation.

John Fremont

John Fremont was an explorer who rode the Oregon Trail in 1842 and 1843. He wanted to encourage people back east to settle the territory. So he wrote reports about how easy the trip was. The reports did excite people into coming west. But John Fremont didn't write most of the reports—his wife, Jessie Benton, did.

Food

Pioneers on the Oregon Trail had to be sure they had enough food for the trip. One settler wrote that he needed "at least 200 pounds of flour, 150 pounds of bacon, 10 pounds of coffee, 20 pounds of sugar, and 10 pounds of salt." A family of four needed about 1,000 pounds of food for the 2,000-mile trip.

1 Why might a person read this chapter?   Lesson 1

   (A) to find out about pioneers on the Oregon Trail

   (B) to find out how to get to Oregon

   (C) to find out interesting facts about Oregon

   (D) to decide whether to move to Oregon

2 The picture, title, and headings tell you that you will read about _____   Lesson 2

   (A) life in Oregon today.

   (B) canals, roads, and trains.

   (C) how pioneers traveled west.

   (D) the 13 original colonies.

3 Why did pioneers probably take the harder overland trip to Oregon?   Lesson 4

   (A) It was less dangerous.

   (B) It took less time.

   (C) It cost less money.

   (D) It was the easiest way.

4 The title helps you to predict that you will learn _____   Lesson 6

   (A) about the first radios and televisions.

   (B) how to build your own covered wagon.

   (C) about schools in early America.

   (D) how pioneers traveled west.

5 You would **not** choose this text if you wanted to _____ Lesson 7

- (A) learn how the pioneers got to Oregon.
- (B) learn what life was like on the Oregon Trail.
- (C) learn how to build your own covered wagon.
- (D) learn what pioneers ate on the trail.

6 The headings tell you that the main idea of this passage is _____

Lesson 10

- (A) how pioneers used the Oregon Trail to move west.
- (B) what life was like in the American colonies.
- (C) how American Indians lived.
- (D) what Oregon is like.

7 *The trip was hard.*
This topic sentence tells you that you will probably learn _____ Lesson 11

- (A) where the Oregon Trail was located.
- (B) why people wanted to move west.
- (C) some of the difficulties pioneers faced on the trail.
- (D) when people stopped using the Oregon Trail.

8 Imagine you are a pioneer on the Oregon Trail. Which of these would you **not** bring with you? _____

Lesson 16

- (A) flour and sugar
- (B) guns
- (C) warm clothes
- (D) delicate china

9 This passage helps you add information about _____ to what you already know about pioneers.

Lesson 19

- (A) life in Texas
- (B) pioneer houses
- (C) life on the Oregon Trail
- (D) how pioneers dressed

10 How could you tell someone the information in the section under the heading *"The Oregon Trail"*? Lesson 14

- (A) Many settlers made the long, hard trip along the Oregon Trail from Missouri to Oregon. These pioneers faced a lot of dangers.
- (B) The worst danger on the trip was cholera. Lightning and wagon accidents were also dangerous.
- (C) The path to Oregon was called the Oregon Trail. Half a million people took this trail from Missouri to Oregon.
- (D) The first people who traveled to Oregon spread the word about how wonderful Oregon was. Soon, many other people decided to move west.

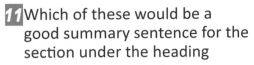

11 Which of these would be a good summary sentence for the section under the heading *"The Pioneers"*? _____ Lesson 15

- (A) People on this expedition spread the news back east about the wonders of Oregon.
- (B) The first trips across the overland route to Oregon led people to spread the news back east about how wonderful Oregon was.
- (C) Jedidiah Smith led the first expedition across the Oregon Trail.
- (D) The path to Oregon took less time than the trip by ship around South America, but it was harder.

12 Which of these would be a good topic sentence for the last paragraph? Lesson 20

- (A) Even though the trip was very hard and dangerous, thousands of pioneers traveled on the Oregon Trail.
- (B) Half a million pioneers took the trail from Missouri to Oregon.
- (C) Some of the dangers the pioneers faced were dangerous streams and rivers, loss of their food, and disease.
- (D) Most of the pioneers on the Oregon Trail rode in large groups of covered wagons.

13 The chapter title tells you that this passage is **mainly** about _____ Lesson 27

- (A) life in today's big cities.
- (B) America's westward expansion.
- (C) the building of Washington, DC.
- (D) the first Constitutional Convention.

14 *The trip was hard.* Which sentence supports this proposition? Lesson 24

- (A) People heard tales about a region of great natural beauty.
- (B) Most men, women, and children left Missouri on covered wagon trains.
- (C) The path to Oregon was called the Oregon Trail.
- (D) Some settlers drowned or lost their belongings in dangerous streams and rivers.

15 What does the picture show? Lesson 25

- (A) what a covered wagon train probably looked like
- (B) how many pioneers went to Oregon
- (C) where most pioneers settled
- (D) how fur traders lived

Questions 16–30: Read the passage and answer the questions. Fill in the letter next to the answer choice you think is correct.

Jeff's Journal

August 23

All I can think about is Color War. That's the biggest event here at Camp Ko-Ko-Ro-Mo. Near the end of every summer, the camp is divided into two teams, the Reds and the Blues. The team that ends up with the most points gets a trophy. Red rules!

The first contest was this afternoon. I hate that the counselors split up Ty and me. It would be great if my best friend were on my team. But we'll stay buddies even though we're enemies, I guess. The problem is, everyone is hanging out just with teammates. It's like you're a traitor if you talk with a Blue.

This afternoon was the swimming competition. I swam in a relay. I was behind in my heat but caught up to Ty and passed him. The Red team won and everyone was high-fiving me. I glanced at Ty, who looked really angry. We shook hands but didn't say much.

The counselors tell us to show sportsmanship. But they also yell at us all the time to beat the other team. In the bunk, we yell, "Red is best!" and they yell back, "Go Blue!" Guys on opposite teams aren't so friendly with each other anymore. It's kind of weird. In the bunk I said, "What's up?" to Ty and he only shrugged.

Still, Red has to win!

August 24

Midmorning we played basketball. Alexa was great. She scored 15 points. I got about 12 rebounds and we crushed the Blues. The total points are in our favor, 45–37. After lunch, I played some games at the computer hut. Some guys from Blue, including Ty, were looking over my shoulder, trying to rattle me. They cheered when I screwed up. I told Ty I could beat him head-to-head at any computer game he picked. But he just laughed at me and walked away with his teammates. I was so angry.

Afternoon: Ping-pong (I'm no good, so I didn't take part); volleyball, which we lost; and archery. I'm no Robin Hood, and Ty beat me badly. I was steaming because I let the team down. I thought I heard Ty diss me, so when he came over to slap me five, I left him hanging. Later, I felt kind of bad. But my Red teammates said I was cool for doing that. Who needs Ty?

August 25

The last day of Color War is the track meet! The teams are close, and after the sprints and relays, we were behind the Blues by five points. So whichever team won the long distance race would also win Color War.

The distance race was brutal. We ran up the main road, around the lake, then into the woods on a marked trail. I got smacked by branches and tripped twice on rocks. Looking back, I saw Ty chugging along. After a while, my lungs felt on fire. I had to stop and bend over. As I did, Ty passed me. I ran as fast as I could and got close to him. We both sprinted to the finish line, both teams screaming like crazy. But Ty beat me by a yard. Maybe two yards. I lost Color War for the Reds.

I felt like two cents. I wanted to hide. Ty came over, said "good race," and stuck his hand out. Because everyone was watching, I gave him a limp handshake and walked away.

Later, I came to realize something. I've made a lot of things in arts and crafts. But the best thing I made at camp was a friend. Who wants to lose friends because of some dumb sports competition? Later, I went to Ty and congratulated him. He put his arm around my shoulder, and we hung out at the snack bar. We were pals again!

16 How did Color War affect Jeff and Ty? *Lesson 3*

- (A) They became friends because they were on the same team.
- (B) They stopped being friends for a while since they were on opposite teams.
- (C) The Color War had no effect on Jeff and Ty.
- (D) They dropped out of the Color War.

17 *Midmorning we played basketball.* Which detail gives more information about this main idea? _____ *Lesson 5*

- (A) Some guys from Blue, including Ty, were looking over my shoulder, trying to rattle me.
- (B) I told Ty I could beat him at any computer game he picked.
- (C) This afternoon was the swimming competition.
- (D) I got about 12 rebounds and we crushed the Blues.

18 Which word might you use to describe Jeff? *Lesson 8*

- (A) greedy
- (B) dishonest
- (C) shy
- (D) athletic

19 Jeff was behind in his heat **before** _____ *Lesson 9*

- (A) Ty caught up to him and passed him.
- (B) the counselors put Jeff and Ty on opposite teams.
- (C) Jeff went to summer camp.
- (D) winning the first contest.

20 *I felt like two cents.* What is this an example of? _____ *Lesson 12*

- (A) personification
- (B) a metaphor
- (C) a simile
- (D) alliteration

21 Which of these events happened **last**? Lesson 13

(A) After a while, my lungs felt on fire.

(B) I got smacked by branches and tripped twice on rocks.

(C) The distance race was brutal.

(D) I lost Color War for the Reds.

22 When Jeff says *"Red rules!"* what does he mean? Lesson 17

(A) The Red team is better than the Blue team.

(B) The Red team makes up the rules for all of the games.

(C) Red is his favorite color.

(D) The rules of the game are written in red.

23 How are basketball and swimming different? Lesson 18

(A) Basketball is a sport, but swimming is not.

(B) Swimming is a sport, but basketball is not.

(C) Jeff's camp offered basketball, but not swimming.

(D) Basketball is played with a ball, but swimming is not.

24 What does the author use to show how hard the competitions were? Lesson 21

(A) persuasion

(B) metaphors such as "the distance race was brutal"

(C) a very formal style

(D) a long list

25 How does Jeff's point of view about Ty change in the story? Lesson 22

(A) He begins by disliking Ty, and then they become friends.

(B) He begins by being afraid of Ty, and then gets the courage to meet Ty.

(C) He and Ty are best friends, and then they become rivals, then become friends again.

(D) Jeff does not change his point of view about Ty.

26 *The Red team won and everyone was high-fiving me.*
Which mental image would help you to understand this part of Jeff's day? Lesson 26

(A) Red team members smiling and giving Jeff high fives

(B) the Red team's jerseys

(C) five Red team members

(D) a trophy

27 Which was the **last** contest? Lesson 28

(A) basketball

(B) archery

(C) track meet

(D) computers

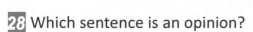

28 Which sentence is an opinion?

Lesson 29

- (A) The last day of Color War is the track meet!
- (B) Midmorning we played basketball.
- (C) But we'll stay buddies even though we're enemies, I guess.
- (D) After lunch, I played some games at the computer hut.

29 Which question does this passage answer?

Lesson 30

- (A) How old is Ty?
- (B) Which sport does Jeff like best?
- (C) How many kids were at camp?
- (D) How many competitions were in Color War?

30 You can conclude that Jeff and Ty will probably _____

Lesson 23

- (A) not see each other again.
- (B) have a fight about Color War.
- (C) remain friends.
- (D) make fun of each other.

Answers

1-5	6-10	11-15	16-20	21-25	26-30
ACBDC	ACDCA	BDDDC	DADBD	BABDA	ACCDC

131

Answer Key

★★ NOTICE ★★

For open-ended questions, answers may vary. The responses listed here are possible answers.

Lesson 01 Purpose for Reading P.6

Part 1

newspapers	magazines
Internet articles	books
signs	cards

Part 2

1. a novel	2. a letter to the editor
3. a newspaper	4. a recipe
5. an essay	6. a math book

Part 3

1. There are a lot of events happening in the community. I focused on the information about karate classes and tryouts for Little League.
2. My purpose for reading this text is to find information about what is happening in the community.

Comprehension Review

1. B   2. D   3. A   4. C   5. B   6. C

Word Power

1. defend   2. recycling   3. volunteer   4. curb

Lesson 02 Previewing P.10

Part 1

YES	
YES	It tells me that the sentences in each paragraph contain related information.
YES	I noticed the title "Harriet Tubman."
	The format tells me that this is a true story.

Part 2

2. Her nickname was Minty.
3. Harriet helped with the Underground Railroad.

Part 3

I have an idea about what Harriet Tubman looked like and about how people dressed in her time.

Comprehension Review

1. B   2. A   3. C   4. C   5. A   6. D

Word Power

1. free state   2. conductor
3. desire   4. plantation

Lesson 03 Cause and Effect—Plot P.14

Part 1

1. The driver had to slam on his brakes to avoid hitting the dog.
2. When it was time for dinner, I was too full to eat.
3. I failed the math test.

Part 2

Cause:
The boy and his grandpa will spend time and money to get the car running.

Effect:
Someday the boy will cruise in the driver's seat of his own car.

Part 3

because	whatever...remember	before you know it

Comprehension Review

1. C   2. B   3. D   4. A   5. B   6. C

Word Power

1. cruise   2. junker
3. vintage   4. repairing

Lesson 04 Making Inferences P. 18

Part 1

My text-to-self connection is that once my cousin left me to get in trouble by myself when we were doing something we shouldn't have been doing.

Part 2

1. The first man was so scared that he didn't think of anything except saving himself.
2. The second man was probably really scared and mad at his friend for leaving him.
3. The second man was probably really mad that his friend was joking about it.
4. The two men might not have been friends anymore after this experience.

Part 3

This passage reminds me of the book *Percy Jackson and the Lightning Thief*. In that story, Percy Jackson is a loyal friend who will not leave behind his friends who are in danger.

Comprehension Review

1. D   2. A   3. C   4. B   5. A   6. C

Word Power

1. nuzzle   2. descend
3. misfortune   4. attack

Lesson 05 Main Idea and Details P. 22

Part 1

Important Fact:

Satyagraha is a philosophy developed by Gandhi.

Insignificant Fact:

Mohandas Gandhi changed his name to Mahatma.

Part 2

1. I am a student.
2. I learn from my mistakes.
3. I like to read.

Part 3

1.	R	2.	I	3.	R
	I		R		I

Comprehension Review

1. B   2. C   3. C   4. A   5. D   6. A

Word Power

1. cause   2. capture
3. threatened   4. support

Lesson 06 Titles and Headings to Predict P. 26

Part 1

I think the "Honeycomb" title means that this passage will include descriptions of bees and hives. The "Perfect Tessellations" might refer to the shapes used to make honeycomb.

Part 2

Most of my predictions were accurate; however, the passage does not describe bees, and it describes tessellations in much greater detail than I predicted before reading.

Comprehension Review

1. C   2. B   3. A   4. D   5. A   6. B

Word Power

1. congruent   2. overlap
3. tessellation   4. repeat

Lesson 07 Selecting Reading Material P. 30

Part 1

I would choose to read about space exploration because it's interesting to learn about how people have journeyed into space.

Part 2

1. My favorite book is *Percy Jackson and the Lightning Thief* because it's interesting, a good story, and hard to put down.
2. My favorite author is Rick Riordan because his books are all good and they make me wish I could be one of his characters.
3. I recommended the *Percy Jackson and the Olympians* series to my friend Zack and my cousin Griffin. I recommended the books because they are good, interesting, and fun to read. I also learned about the Greek gods while reading this series.

4. I don't enjoy reading boring books about things I
   don't care about.
5. I used to like reading silly stories and science
   fiction. Now, I like reading nonfiction books about
   battles and warriors.

Part 3
The book by Rick Riordan titled *Percy Jackson and the
Lightning Thief* is great reading! The characters are
interesting, they have epic battles to save the world,
and Riordan makes you want to join their camp and
become a half-blood. It is the first in a series about
the half-god Percy Jackson, and if you like it, you'll
probably enjoy reading the entire series.

Comprehension Review
1. C   2. B   3. D   4. A   5. A   6. B

Word Power
1. satellite   2. cosmonaut
3. mission   4. launch

Lesson 08 Character Development
P. 34

Part 1
The following words and phrases from the passage
helped me understand the character: tall, skinny,
imposing; blond hair; sparkling blue eyes; powerhouse
on the basketball court; a gazelle; helped his little
sister; loved history; spent hours reading.

Part 2
1. I imagined that I saw Johnny, and he was tall and
   skinny with blond hair and wearing a basketball
   uniform.
2. I imagined smelling the grass as he mowed the
   lawn every weekend.
3. I imagined hearing Johnny on the phone at night,
   laughing about his day.
4. I imagined touching a basketball net while doing a
   slam dunk.

Part 3
I learned that Johnny is an extraordinary person; a
great athlete; and a generous, kind, and helpful family
member.

Comprehension Review
1. A   2. C   3. B   4. D   5. C   6. A

Word Power
1. soar   2. mischief   3. agility   4. imposing

Lesson 09 Logical Order P. 38

Part 1
I read a set of directions, called a *recipe*, and it helped
me make a pie.

Part 2
1. People have been using hydroponics for thousands
   of years.
2. I should place the pot where it will receive lots of
   sunlight.
3. The plants are grown in water instead of soil.
4. It's hard to say how deep I should plant my seeds,
   but I'm sure that I shouldn't plant the seeds too
   deeply.

Part 3
1. B	6. B
2. E	7. F
3. A	8. C
4. D	9. E
5. C	10. D

Comprehension Review
1. B   2. D   3. C   4. A   5. B   6. A

Word Power
1. fray   2. fertilizer   3. effective   4. insert

Lesson 10 Headings to Determine
         Main Ideas P. 42

Part 1
Headings might be included to give more information.

Part 2
I might read about all of the great things that
Benjamin Franklin did in his lifetime.

Part 3

A Writer
Question:
Why was Benjamin Franklin a great writer?
Predicted Answer:
He probably wrote something important.

A Politician
Question:
What did Benjamin Franklin do as a politician?
Predicted Answer:
He probably helped his people as a politician.

Serving His Country
Question:
How did Benjamin Franklin serve his country?
Predicted Answer:
He probably served his country by making lots of contributions to literature and politics.

Comprehension Review

1. C   2. B   3. D   4. A   5. B   6. D

Word Power

1. document   2. diplomat
3. fulfill   4. almanack

Lesson 11 Topic Sentences to Predict P. 46

Part 1

I predict that this passage will discuss predators and their prey.

Part 2

The passage is about food chains and food webs. The author describes how organisms are dependent on one another.

Part 3

2. Green plants are called *producers* in the chain of life.
3. Consumers are the living organisms that get energy from eating others.

Comprehension Review

1. A   2. C   3. B   4. A   5. D   6. C

Word Power

1. consumer   2. interdependence
3. photosynthesis   4. release

Lesson 12 Literary Devices P. 50

Part 1

I was thinking about what it would feel like to live in that city on that day. I thought of how sweaty and warm I would feel and how I would like to drink a glass of lemonade.

Part 2

Thump!	Craaaak!	Wham!
Clunk!	Ring!	Rooaaar!

Part 3

2. The city air rises up in a zigzag.
3. Light bounces off the cars.
4. Dark storm clouds roll ominously.

Comprehension Review

1. B   2. D   3. C   4. A   5. B   6. C

Word Power

1. devour   2. sweltering
3. monotonous   4. labor

Lesson 13 Sequential Order P. 54

Part 1

The narrator told this in sequential order because he wanted to show the increasingly ridiculous steps the narrator took to turn off the alarm.

Part 2

then	now	as

Part 3

1. The alarm clock rings.
2. The narrator tries different ways to turn off the alarm.
3. The narrator finally succeeds in turning off the alarm.
4. The narrator goes back to sleep.

Comprehension Review
1. A   2. C   3. B   4. A   5. D   6. B

Word Power
1. tingly   2. resounding   3. surrender   4. hysterically

Lesson 14 Paraphrasing P. 58

Part 1

Summary of the beginning of the passage:
The land belonging to the Lakota Indians contained gold, prompting people to travel through the territory to get it.

Summary of the middle of the passage:
The Bozeman Trail caused problems for the Lakota Indians, and the U.S. government's response angered them further and led to Red Cloud's War.

Summary of the end of the passage:
Later, the Lakota Indians found themselves dealing with the same problem, which led to a war with General George Custer. The Indians won the battle.

Part 2

The Lakota, an American Indian tribe from the northern Great Plains, had a strong history of protecting their land against outsiders. The first settlers and the Indians were able to share the land and its resources; however, when the Bozeman Trail was built through Lakota territory, hunting and fishing became difficult for the Lakota. They began attacking travelers on the trail.

The U.S. government got involved, but even during the meeting with the Lakota chief, Red Cloud, the army was building forts along the trail. Red Cloud and the other Lakota attacked the forts, and the army eventually left and closed the trail. After this, the Lakota and the U.S. government signed a treaty, setting aside Lakota land.

However, in 1874, when gold was found on Lakota land, miners from all over the country invaded, and the government offered to buy the land. The Lakota refused, and there was a war. Sitting Bull was the Lakota chief and General George Custer was the leader of the U.S. Army. The Lakota were successful in defending their land.

Comprehension Review
1. A   2. A   3. A   4. D   5. A   6. D

Word Power
1. sacred   2. reservation
3. official   4. invade

Lesson 15 Summary Sentences P. 62

Part 1

Fact 1:
Abolitionists thought all slaves should be free.

Fact 2:
Abolitionists organized the Underground Railroad.

Fact 3:
Abolitionists would contact slaves who wanted to escape and would tell them where to go first on the route to the North.

Part 2

1. I think that abolitionists did what they felt was the right thing and helped slaves escape to freedom in the North.
2. My reaction didn't change after reading the summary sentence.

Part 3

The author's main idea is that abolitionists risked their own lives to help slaves escape to freedom through the Underground Railroad.

Comprehension Review
1. B   2. A   3. A   4. D   5. B   6. A

Word Power
1. swamp   2. route
3. force   4. debate

5

Lesson 16 Reflecting on What Has Been Learned P. 66

Part 1
This passage made me think about how lucky Wade and his family are to be able to design their own house. This means they will get the house they really want.

Part 2
I can relate to this passage because I just painted my own room and moved the furniture around. I got to make all the decisions and set things up the way I wanted them.

Part 3
My dream home would be made of bricks. It would be big enough for everyone in my family to have his or her own room.

Comprehension Review
1. C   2. B   3. A   4. C   5. D   6. B

Word Power
1. composed   2. geometry
3. architect   4. design

Lesson 17 Use of Language P. 70

Part 1
I think the language is so descriptive that I could almost see and hear what was happening in the story.

Part 2
2. I was a knight who had conquered the dragon.
3. hands like vulture's claws
4. hair looks like a tangle of thorns

Part 3
I think the dialogue adds a lot to the story. It tells me that the sisters do not get along and that the mom is very kind and understanding.

Comprehension Review
1. A   2. D   3. B   4. C   5. A   6. B

Word Power
1. sinister   2. tangled
3. dejected   4. chameleon

Lesson 18 Compare and Contrast P. 74

Part 1
I think the author chose a compare-and-contrast text structure because the biomes have similarities and differences that are important to point out to the reader.

Part 2

Tundra	• has permafrost • no trees • home to polar bears, snowy owls, caribou, and wolves
Both	• very cold • northernmost part of the world
Taiga	• largest land biome • has evergreen trees • home to birds and deer

Part 3
Other topics that would be appropriate for a compare-and-contrast text include a comparison of frogs and toads, a discussion about the works of Dr. Seuss and Maurice Sendak, and descriptions of the different continents.

Comprehension Review
1. C   2. D   3. B   4. A   5. C   6. B

Word Power
1. lichen   2. temperate
3. shrub   4. tundra

Lesson 19 Adjust and Extend Knowledge P. 78

Part 1
I thought I knew everything about how to play soccer, and then I read a biography of a famous soccer player and realized how hard he works to be good at the game. It made me look at the sport in a new way.

Part 2

I know that biodiversity refers to the many different kinds of life on Earth.

Part 3

The part of the text that surprised me was that van Roosmalen is a biologist who studies spider monkeys. I was also surprised to learn that new species of monkey are still being discovered.

Comprehension Review

1. A   2. C   3. B   4. D   5. C   6. B

Word Power

1. biodiversity   2. conservation
3. species   4. expert

Lesson 20 Topic Sentences to Determine Main Ideas P. 82

Part 1
My Prediction

The passage will describe other features of the velociraptor and how it hunted.

Part 2
What the Passage Is About

The passage describes how velociraptor looks like and how do those features benefit it to catch preys.

Part 3
Detail 2:

It had long fingers with sharp claws, perfect for holding on to struggling prey.

Detail 3:

The tail also may have helped it change direction quickly while sprinting after its supper.

Comprehension Review

1. C   2. A   3. C   4. D   5. A   6. D

Word Power

1. paleontologist   2. sprint
3. hunter   4. predatory

Lesson 21 Author's Devices P. 86

Part 1

I think the author uses an interesting story to teach the reader a lesson because it demonstrates how working together makes tasks easier. Using an example readers can relate to is more effective than simply telling them what to do.

Part 2
Author's Purpose:

The author's purpose is to teach the reader a lesson.

Text Clues:

Each of the sons tries, but fails, the challenge. Then the father teaches them how to work together to complete the task.

Part 3

The devices the author uses include dialogue, vivid verbs, repetition, a clear explanation of the lesson learned by the sons, and so on.

Comprehension Review

1. B   2. C   3. A   4. D   5. A   6. C

Word Power

1. prosper   2. devise   3. inherit   4. quarrel

Lesson 22 Author's Point of View P. 90

Part 1

The point of view of this passage is first person. I think the author chose this point of view to make the story more personal. This helps the reader understand the narrator's thoughts and feelings and makes the story more interesting.

Part 2

Yesterday, I was skateboarding on the sidewalk near my house, and all of a sudden, a dog started chasing me as if I were a bone with wheels. He was barking so loudly that I thought my eardrums would explode. All I could think about was getting out of his way, but my feet wouldn't cooperate. They didn't want to move. Probably no more than three seconds passed before I snapped out of it. I jumped on my skateboard, and it whisked me away to the safety of my front porch.

Part 3

Yesterday, Jason was skateboarding on the sidewalk near his house, and all of a sudden, a dog started chasing him as if he were a bone with wheels. The dog was barking so loudly that Jason thought his eardrums would explode. All he could think about was getting out of the dog's way, but his feet wouldn't cooperate. They didn't want to move. Probably no more than three seconds passed before Jason snapped out of it. He jumped on his skateboard, and it whisked him away to the safety of his front porch.

Comprehension Review

1. D   2. B   3. A   4. C   5. B   6. A

Word Power

1. generosity   2. cherish   3. visit   4. tousle

Lesson 23 Drawing Conclusions P. 94

Part 1

This is a formal letter written to a person whom the author does not know well.

Part 2

Explicit Information:

Freda's Flower Shop is located in Tulip, TN.

Implicit Information:

Elvina likes learning the meaning of different names.

Part 3

1. The sender likes Freda because she says Freda has a calming nature.
2. The sender enjoys sharing information about people's names.
3. The author wants the reader to understand how to set up a business letter.
4. I think Elvina is an interesting person because she enjoys researching names.

Comprehension Review

1. B   2. B   3. A   4. D   5. B   6. C

Word Power

1. correspond   2. mannerism   3. unhurried   4. reflect

Lesson 24 Proposition and Support P. 98

Part 1

Proposition:
Authors are talented, special people.

Support:
The supports includes *articulate, capacity for empathy, respect the power of words, share themselves with others.*

Part 2

It is everyone's job to clean up trash and keep the school clean.

Reason #1: Students and staff need to work together for the good of the school.

Reason #2: Cleaning up the school is too big of a job for just one person.

Reason #3: Putting trash where it belongs shows respect for the environment and the school.

Comprehension Review

1. A   2. C   3. B   4. D   5. C   6. A

Word Power

1. empathy   2. articulate   3. envy   4. reach

Lesson 25 Graphic Features P. 102

Part 1

Graphic features can help the reader by providing a visual representation of what the author is explaining. Graphic features also help the reader locate information quickly and can provide a comprehension check.

Part 2

Fact 1:
The retina is at the back of the eye.
Fact 2:
The cornea is the front part of the eye
Fact 3:
The eye sees things upside down.

Part 3

The graphic features helped me see what was being described in the text. For example, when I read the clause "After light enters the pupil," I knew where the pupil was thanks to the drawings.

Comprehension Review

1. B   2. C   3. A   4. C   5. D   6. B

Word Power

1. iris   2. retina
3. cornea   4. pupil

Lesson 26 Mental Images P. 106

Part 1

The picture of the seal helps me understand the Aztec prophecy.

Part 2

What did you see?	
I saw floating highways.	
What did you hear?	
I heard warriors yelling in battle.	
What did you smell?	
I smelled hot chilies.	
What did you feel?	
I felt the cool lake water.	

Part 3

1. The Aztecs decided to settle there because it matched the sun god's prophecy.
2. The location was perfect because it was good for farming and it provided safety from their enemies.
3. They created floating gardens in the marshland.
4. The Aztecs were good farmers, engineers, athletes, and scientists.

Comprehension Review

1. C   2. B   3. D   4. A   5. C   6. B

Word Power

1. invincible   2. empire   3. marshland   4. canal

Lesson 27 Chapter Titles to Determine Main Ideas P. 110

Part 1

Before Reading
I wonder how germs spread? What are protozoa?
During Reading
They can enter through the mouth, nose, or other openings; most times our bodies are able to fight germs; protozoa are a type of germ.
After Reading
I learned that our bodies can mostly fight all types of germs, but certain people, like children, are more likely to get sick because the adult body is better at fighting infections.
Further Reading
I still want to know exactly how germs get into the body through the openings and what the germs do once they get in.

Part 2

The main idea of this chapter is what diseases are and how they are spread.

Part 3

Germs Everywhere!	World of Germs	Germs All Over!

Comprehension Review

1. A   2. C   3. C   4. D   5. C   6. A

Word Power

1. fungi   2. virus   3. bacteria   4. infection

Lesson 28 Chronological Order P. 114

Part 1

This text presents the events in chronological order, or as they happened in history.

Part 2

The type of structure that makes the most sense for this passage is chronological order. I think it is easy to understand a historical topic when it is described from beginning to end, but I guess it depends on the topic, too.

Part 3

1. Five dynasties are described in this passage.
2. The Qin was the shortest, the Zhou was the longest, and the Han was the strongest.
3. The Great Wall was built to protect the territories.
4. The Silk Road linked Asia and Europe.

Comprehension Review

1. C   2. B   3. D   4. A   5. C   6. B

Word Power

1. emperor   2. territory
3. reign   4. dynasty

Lesson 29 Fact and Opinion P. 118

Part 1
Fact:
The president of the United States attended this school 40 years ago.

Opinion:
What an opportunity for me!

Part 2

Bananas

Fact:
Bananas are yellow.

Opinion:
Bananas taste good.

Rock and Roll

Fact:
Rock and roll is a type of music.

Opinion:
Rock and roll is fun to dance to.

Bicycles

Fact:
Bicycles have two wheels.

Opinion:
Bikes are an easy way to get around town.

Cats

Fact:
Cats walk on four legs.

Opinion:
Cats are lovely companions.

Comprehension Review

1. A   2. C   3. B   4. C   5.C   6. B

Word Power

1. intently   2. delusional
3. duration   4. overhear

Lesson 30 Questioning P. 122

Part 1
2. What test is the girl taking?
3. Which class is the test in?
4. Is the girl well prepared for the test?

Part 2

Large Question:
Why didn't Kiley tell the teacher about Lola?

Small Question:
Did any of the other kids notice Lola cheating?

Part 3

A fact about the topic:
Plants can grow in water rather than soil.

Question for a Friend:
Would you want a hydroponic garden?

Question for the Author:
How did you learn about hydroponics?

Comprehension Review

1. D   2. A   3.C   4. B   5.A   6. C

Word Power

1. screech   2. respond
3. review   4. resound

Lesson 01　社區訊息公告欄 P.4

小聯盟徵選
這個星期六下午一點
更多訊息請撥 555-2941 洽布萊德
請自備手套

合唱團練習
每個星期三，晚上七點半
第十街的浸禮會教堂
交誼廳集合

義消薄煎餅餐會
星期六
5PM ~ 7PM

搬家大拍賣
東園街 56 號
出售家具、玩具、衣服，和一台腳踏車
洗衣機、乾衣機兩台 $100

注意
資源回收日已變更，現在改為星期三。
請在早上八點前將回收物品放到人行道的路邊。

馬簑公園狗狗美容
帶你的狗來，讓我們幫牠洗澎澎
洗一隻狗五塊錢，除蟲另計
如果需要更多資訊，請打 555-0971 找麗莎詢問

空手道班
黑帶級老師
每週兩次，星期三和星期四，晚上六點
除了學會保護自己，也來點樂子吧！

Lesson 02　海麗特‧塔布曼 P.8

海麗特‧塔布曼出生於 1820 年左右，當時她被命名為亞諾曼塔‧羅斯，而她的小名叫薄荷。長大後，人們不再叫她薄荷，改叫她海麗特，這同時也是她母親的名字，而她的父親人稱老班。

海麗特在馬里蘭州東岸的一個農場長大。她和父母都是農場的奴隸，而海麗特之所以為奴隸，正是因為父母是奴隸。她有很多兄弟姐妹，其中有幾位在其他的農場工作。

海麗特還小時，白天她和其他的孩子一起玩耍。當她的父母在田野工作時，一位年長的婦人就負責看顧他們。

晚上，海麗特就睡在小屋的泥地上。有時候她會聽大人談論自由，雖然她不知道自由是什麼，但是她覺得那聽起來很棒，也想知道更多相關的事。七歲時，海麗特試著要逃離農場，可是她並沒有成功。

海麗特聽到自由這個詞時非常地好奇，等她大到可以了解自由是甚麼意思的時候，她也想要自由。海麗特試著和母親討論自由，但母親卻很怕聽到這事。不過她的父親倒很樂意談論它，老班希望自己的女兒能夠做好獲得自由的準備。

1844 年，海麗特嫁給了自由之人——約翰‧塔布曼，這讓海麗特更想獲得自由了。可是約翰並不希望海麗特逃跑，但海麗特的父親卻持相反的意見。老班教海麗特怎麼在樹林中生活，因為老班覺得她得知道如何生存。他教導她如何追隨北極星的方向，怎麼游泳和生火。她學會捕捉動物的方法，也學會如何剝去動物皮以便食用。

海麗特計畫逃亡好幾次，但每次都因為時機不對，所以沒有行動。1849 那年，她發現自己可能要被賣掉，她相信逃離的時候到了。

沿途有很多人幫助海麗特。在躲躲藏藏好幾日後，她終於成功地到達解放奴隸的賓州。海麗特在賓州的費城找到了一份工作。她努力工作，並且存了錢，憑著一份幫助其他奴隸的渴望，她成了「地下鐵路組織」的首位女性領導者。

Lesson 03　盯緊目標 P.12

我 14 歲時，老爸買了一台很棒的舊老爺車給我。車體的狀況還算是不錯，但零件需要整修一番。老爸提醒我比爾爺爺很喜歡修補舊車，如果我能有禮貌地請求他，他或許可以幫我修這部老爺車。「在你拿到駕照前，還有兩年的時間可以修理它。」老爸說，「這應該可以給你足夠的時間來讓它上路了，不過零件的部分你得用自己的錢，因為我已經盡我所能花錢買這部車了。」

你可以想像我是多麼地興奮，因為我才 14 歲就有自己的車了！而且還不是隨便一輛車，這可是一台活動摺篷車呢！還有什麼能比這更酷的呢？除此之外，有件事情也讓我超開心，那就是這部車跟我同年出生。呃，好吧，車子不能算是出生……因為它們是被製造出來的。不過你懂的。

隔天，爺爺來了後，他往後一站，仔細地評估我的「老藍仔」，這是我為這部車取的名字。「它的外表看起來還差強人意。」爺爺終於開口說，「但是要看看車體內部的狀況才知道它到底如何。我們把車抬起來檢查一下，你去拿個東西記下來，我會告訴你之後需要的東西。」

我迅速地拿了筆記本和鉛筆，回去的時候，我發現爺爺已經把車子架高了。「有些修理的部分，我們可以自己來，也就是說你只需要買零件。但是其他主要的部分就得在艾迪的車廠進行了，你知道去車廠修的話會有點貴。」他退了一步，站了一會兒。他把手搭在我的肩上道：「不管要付出多少錢和多少努力，記得一心一意地想著你的目標，想像你坐在駕駛座上，開著自己的車，到處兜風。然後不知不覺中，你就會辦到了。」

Lesson 04 熊與兩個旅人 P. 16

這是一個有關兩個結伴同行的旅人，在前往目的地的途中穿越樹林時的故事。有隻熊突然出現在路中，擋在他們面前威嚇他們。

第一個人：「我不假思索，立刻爬上一棵樹，躲進枝葉中保護自己。」

第二個人：「我跟著我的旅伴這麼做，可是我卻絆倒了。我知道我可能馬上就會被攻擊，所以我躺在地上一動也不動。」

第一個人：「我從藏身的安全地點看著那隻熊。牠探觸躺在地上的人，用牠的鼻子嗅他，摩擦他全身。」

第二個人：「我屏住呼吸裝死。」

據說熊不會攻擊屍體，所以那隻熊很快就離開了。確定熊已經離開後，另一個旅人從樹上下來，開玩笑地問了他朋友一個問題。

第一個人：「那隻熊跟你說了什麼悄悄話啊？」

第二個人：「牠給我一個忠告：絕對不要和一個在危險來臨就遺棄你的朋友一起旅行。」

這個故事的寓意就是：不幸能考驗朋友的誠意。

Lesson 05 偉大的靈魂——聖雄甘地 P. 20

1915 年，穆漢達‧甘地和他的家人回到了印度。甘地開始建造活動中心，讓人們學習他的生活方式，他希望人們能為自己的社區服務。此外，他的不合作主義也獲得人們的支持。不合作主義是一種由甘地所創的哲學，或者說一種思考方式。

當時印度仍在英國的統治之下，許多英國律法對印度人並不公平。甘地教導人們以不合作主義來改變不平等的事，他們也努力不懈的堅持著。在 1919 年，新律法奪走了印度人更多的自由。當時被稱為聖雄的穆漢達‧甘地開始對抗法律。他受到所有的印度人，以及世界上許多人的矚目。自此，印度的人們開始為自己國家的獨立而努力。

甘地待在印度的這段時間發生了許多重要事件，其中一件就是 1930 年的鹽稅長征。英國對印度人課鹽稅，而且只有英國人能夠製鹽。因此甘地帶領一大群人進行遊行示威，他們走了 165 英里到達阿拉伯海。在那裡，他們以蒸發海水的方式製鹽。

甘地常受到威脅與牢獄之災，但他仍然不放棄他的工作。1947 年，他證明了不合作主義的力量，在經過英國 200 年的統治後，印度終於成為一個自由的國家。

Lesson 06 蜂巢 P. 24

蜜蜂棲息在蜂窩裡，而這些蜂窩常可以在中空的樹木中發現。蜂窩裡有蜂巢，蜂巢是由很多稱為巢室的 3D 形體所構成，蜜蜂將蜂蜜和幼蟲放置在這些巢室中。

每一個蜂巢都是六角柱。這個六角柱的命名來自它兩邊底部的形狀——六角形，是有六個邊的 2D 形狀。蜂巢的六角形組成幾何圖形，這些圖形之間沒有任何的空隙，也沒有重疊的部分。

像這樣的圖形稱為密鋪平面（tessellations）。密鋪平面就是用同一種圖形，不斷地在平面上重複拼砌，不留任何空隙也沒有重疊之處。密鋪平面這個字指的就是以棋盤式或馬賽克式的排列方法，排列小方塊。Tessellate 這個字源自希臘文 tesseres，意思是「四」。一個正多邊形有三個、四個、五個，甚至更多對等的邊和角。一個正密鋪平面是由全等的正多邊形所組成，這裡「正」的意思是指這個多邊形的邊都等長，而「全等」是指所有放在一起的多邊形都是相等的大小和形狀。

完美的密鋪平面

只有三種形狀能夠構成完美的密鋪平面，分別是正方形、等邊三角形和正六邊形。

Lesson 07　太空之旅 P. 28

1957 年，蘇聯發射史普尼克一號，太空競賽就此揭開序幕。史普尼克一號是史上第一架人造衛星。四年後，蘇聯太空人賈加林成了第一位駕駛太空船的人。

如今最大的太空研究機構在美國，也就是美國太空總署（NASA）。NASA 的阿波羅 11 號任務讓美國成了第一個將人類送上月球的國家。1969 年，太空人阿姆斯壯成為第一位在月球上漫步的人。他在月球上說了句名言，他說：「我的一小步，是人類的一大步。」

NASA 後來創造了太空梭，也就是可以重複使用的太空船。從 1981 年至今，太空梭艦隊已經出了一百多次任務。令人遺憾的是，有兩名隊員在不幸的意外中喪命。

1983 年，太空探測船先鋒 10 號成了第一個離開太陽系的人造物體，不過它是 11 年前發射的！

我們的太空基地

你知道有個實驗室在外太空漂浮著嗎？它被稱為國際太空站，簡稱 ISS，是夜空中最明亮的物體之一。它就像一個在外太空的家，太空人住在那裡，並且進行實驗。來自 16 個不同國家的人曾在那工作，而太空站裡一直有至少兩個人在裡面待命。第一批機組員在 2000 年抵達，而大多數的機組員會待上六個月左右的時間。

太空計畫的未來

太空探險的未來會如何？ NASA 未來的計畫將帶領我們到達新的頂點。下一個送人類到月球的旅行計畫預計在 2018 年執行，任務期程約七天。科學家希望太空人能夠創造出水、燃料以及其他維持生命的必需品。如此一來，在月球上建立家園便指日可待了。除此之外，還有計畫要讓太空人在 2028 年前造訪火星。這會是一個耗時較長的任務，太空人將在火星表面停留 500 天。

冥王星也會受到來自地球的拜訪。冥王星是太陽系邊緣的一顆矮行星。2006 年一月，NASA 發射新視界號，展開一段非常漫長的旅程，預計在 2015 年抵達冥王星。這艘沒有載人的太空船將繞行冥王星，並傳送畫面和數據資料回地球。新視界號必定會為我們帶來驚喜，幫助我們更了解太陽系和宇宙。

Lesson 08　飛躍強尼 P. 32

高、消瘦、令人印象深刻──這是強尼的朋友對他的描述。強尼的金髮都會用一點髮膠固定，這樣它才能維持整天不變型。他總是做最潮的打扮，大大的 T 恤、寬鬆的短褲，還有昂貴的運動鞋。不過女生們最愛的還是他那雙透露了淘氣的閃亮藍眼睛。

強尼在籃球場上也是一座發電廠。有人說他可以從一千英呎（304.8 公尺）遠的地方進籃。他的敏捷讓他可以在球場上跳躍、閃躲與舞動。在活動中，他是一頭瞪羚，毫不費力地往目標前進。在球場上，他的朋友稱他「飛躍強尼」。他之所以得到這個稱號，是因為他能夠跳到空中大約十英呎高的位置，將球灌進籃網中，然後平穩落地，隨後又在場上飛快地繼續下一波攻勢。

在家時，飛躍強尼既不調皮也不飛躍。他幫妹妹看功課，也幫忙擺設餐桌，暑假的週末還幫忙除草。他喜歡歷史，每個晚上總是花上好幾個小時，閱讀著名的戰役和美國歷任總統的書。但是當他的朋友一呼喚，他又表現出在學校的樣子來了。他會暢談大笑，還會開玩笑來表現出他並沒有將生活看得太嚴肅，他知道接下來的日子會有更多有趣和冒險的事。

Lesson 09 水耕法 P. 36

「不用土壤種植物,這聽起來根本就是胡說八道。」我的姑姑艾瑪不相信的驚呼,「我從來沒見過沒有肥沃黑土的園圃。」

「這是我們今天在課堂上學到的。」我解釋道,「這叫水耕法——用水代替土壤來種東西,人們已經這樣做好幾千年了。妳看,這是所需物品的清單和做法。」我把那天從老師那拿來的操作說明遞給她看。「我想要在水耕的環境下種植物,來當做我今年的科學報告。如果您能幫我的話,我會非常的感激,因為您是種植東西的專家啊。」

你需要:

· 廣口瓶
· 免洗杯
· 一段棉繩
· 種子
· 蛭石
· 水耕肥料

怎麼做:

1. 取一段與瓶子等長的棉繩,把繩子的兩端磨一下,做出繩蕊來。

2. 在杯底戳一個洞,把繩子穿過杯中的洞。把蛭石裝進杯子時,要把杯子拿好。

3. 將水耕肥料和水混合做出可用的植物養料。

4. 把恰當份量的養料水倒入瓶中,以保麗龍杯塞進瓶頸時,養料水的高度不碰到杯底為原則。

5. 將保麗龍杯塞進瓶頸,讓繩蕊垂掛浸泡在養料水中。

6. 把種子放進蛭石堆中(不要太深)。

7. 把罐子放在可以接收到大量陽光的地方。

姑姑有協助我做這個科學報告。有天她對我說:「你知道嗎,這水耕栽種唯一的缺點就是,你的手永遠不會弄髒!」

Lesson 10 班傑明 · 富蘭克林: 一位偉人之死 P. 40

班傑明 · 富蘭克林死於 1790 年 4 月 17 日。在他 1738 年所著的《窮查理年鑑》中,富蘭克林寫道:「如果你不想一死掉發臭就被人遺忘,要不就寫點值得人家看的東西,要不就做點值得人家寫的事情。」富蘭克林也的確實踐了自己的話,他是一位偉大的作家,也是一位很棒的實踐者。

作家

富蘭克林年輕時,他寫給編輯的有趣信件讓當地的報紙大賣。他藉由預測競爭對手的死亡,讓自己的年鑑成為暢銷書。雖然他的對手並沒有真的死去,但鎮民們都愛死了這本年鑑。然而,富蘭克林不只是一個頗具創意的作家,他還協助撰寫了美國歷史中最重要的兩份文件,一份是《獨立宣言》,另一份則是美國憲法。

政治家

富蘭克林同時也是位老練的政治家。費城人民選他為英國議會的代表,不久後,其他的殖民地也請他做為他們的外交代表。回到故鄉後,他在獨立戰爭中支持殖民地獨立。隨後,美國國會送他到法國去。法國人很喜歡富蘭克林,在法國他被當成名人一樣受到款待。由於富蘭克林的關係,法國人幫助殖民地贏得了戰爭。在戰爭尾聲,他也致力於與英國和平協商的工作。

為國服務

富蘭克林不僅是一位作家和政治家。他研究電學、創辦圖書館,也蓋了醫院。富蘭克林還成立了費城第一個消防隊和警隊。就許多方面而言,他的確是政績卓越。

Lesson 11 生命的相互依賴 P. 44

綠色植物在生物鏈中被稱為生產者。它們利用二氧化碳、水、礦物質和陽光生產所需的能量，其能量是單一型態的糖類，讓植物可以生長。

在光合作用的過程中，植物透過葉子釋放出氧氣與水分。生產者很重要，因為它們不只提供能量給自己，也提供能量給其他生物。

消費者是透過吃掉其他生物以得到能量的生物，動物可以吃掉植物或其他動物獲得維持生命的能量。分解者協助分解生物的屍體，它們分解樹葉、木頭與動物，幫助生命繼續循環。

在群落中，生物居住在一起，互相傳遞能量，稱為食物鏈。舉例來說，植物可能被昆蟲吃掉，而昆蟲可能被鳥兒吃掉，鳥兒可能被蛇吃掉，然後蛇可能被老鷹吃掉。

食物鏈組成食物網，食物鏈中的植物或動物也可能被連結到另一個食物鏈中。舉例來說，昆蟲可能同時是青蛙與蛇兩條食物鏈的一部分。群落中的食物網是由許多食物鏈構成。

在食物鏈中不同階層的生物，都可以得到生命所需的能量。生產者，也就是綠色植物，擁有最多的能量，有些能量會用在植物自身上，因為它們需要能量生長和進行光合作用。植物被吃掉後，部分能量就會傳遞下去。動物吃下植物，從植物中獲得能量，這些能量可以幫助動物維持生命，讓身體繼續運作。當動物被吃掉後，那些保存在動物體內的能量就會傳遞給下一個動物。生物鏈如同金字塔一般，最底層能量最多，而最頂層的能量最少。

人類能影響食物鏈及食物網。舉例來說，森林被清除後，生產者與消費者都會受到影響。樹木是生產者，森林中其他的消費者和生產者可能從樹上獲取所需的能量，清除土地以建造新的城市或高速公路，會破壞原本居住在那裡的群落。

Lesson 12 城市的夏天 P. 48

想像一個炎熱的夏天，太陽直直照射在柏油路上，城市中的空氣蜿蜒地上升著，光線反射在停在路邊的車上。有一度，整個社區唯一可以聽到的聲音就是風扇傳來規律的嗡嗡聲，努力的讓住戶們可以從悶熱的氣溫中涼快些。

無聊的孩子們決定勇敢的面對潮濕的熱氣，到街上玩球。砰！砰！砰！籃球重複的聲響打破了一成不變的寂靜。孩子進進出出的跳著、移動著、閃躲著、嘻笑著，來去自如，在炎炎夏日中玩耍。

發出挑動神經旋律的冰淇淋車出現了。孩子們興奮的跑到車子邊，挑選冰淇淋口味—香草甜筒、巧克力脆棒，以及色彩繽紛的冰棒。孩子們一下子就吃光光了，繼續活力十足的玩耍。

暴風雨的烏雲如惡兆般席捲過頭頂上的天空，街道空了，陰鬱的灰像把巨傘籠罩整個天空。砰的一聲！遠處閃電急舞，雷聲隨之怒吼。大雨如注，劈哩啪啦的打在人行道、街道與屋瓦上。一張張臉好奇的望著窗外，觀看這場令人頭暈目眩的表演。當烏雲散去，蒸汽升起，街道乾了，另一場嬉戲又再度上演。

Lesson 13 鬧鐘 P. 52

我被鬧鐘的聲響叫醒，我知道我馬上就得去上學。鬧鐘在房間的另一頭鈴鈴地響著，我站在床邊的地板上，揉揉眼睛，睡眼惺忪地走向鬧鐘。當我笨拙的將手伸向鬧鐘時，發現雙手有一點點刺痛的感覺，隨後兩隻手就都毫無感覺了。因為昨晚睡覺的時候，我的兩隻手都被壓在身子底下，現在沒有一隻手動得了。我試著用重如千斤的手關掉鬧鐘，但是鬧鐘仍然響個不停。左手和右手一樣無動於衷。

我歇斯底里的笑著，傾身彎向鬧鐘，試著用鼻子去按按鍵，但我的鼻子擠不進那小小的地方。我試著用手肘關，但它也太大了。我試著坐在上面，不過完全沒用。我倒在床上，舉起我的腳，試著用腳趾頭去戳鬧鐘按鈕。全都沒用！鬧鐘還是不停的響。

我向鈴聲舉旗投降，決定等一等。我拖著腳步穿過走廊走進廚房，響亮的鬧鈴聲傳遍屋子。我的雙手慢慢地恢復知覺，我立刻衝過走廊，爬上樓梯跑回房間，焦急的按掉鬧鐘。

寂靜竟是如此美妙！從過去的經驗我知道，如果一天是這樣開始的話，就該再回去睡覺，而我也打算這麼做。當我在睡回籠覺時，我突然想到今天鬧鐘響這麼久是件比平常還糟糕的事，因為今天是星期六啊！

Lesson 14 　1800 年代的美國印地安人 P. 56

拉科塔族的印地安人居住在北美大平原區，也就是現今美國的北達柯他州、南達柯他州、蒙大拿州、懷俄明州，以及加拿大的阿爾伯塔省、曼尼托巴省和薩斯喀徹溫省，提供印地安人與殖民者許多美洲野牛。在這個地區發現金礦之前，白人殖民者都不曾干擾過印地安人。

兩位山地人（mountain man）規劃了一條稱為「博茲曼小道」（Bozeman Trail）的路線，穿過拉科塔地區。大批金礦礦工開始在這條路線上往返。

一位名叫紅雲（Red Cloud）的拉科塔酋長希望能關閉博茲曼小道，因為礦工和運貨的馬車擾亂了美洲野牛的作息，使得打獵變得更困難了。拉科塔人開始恐嚇每個走那條路線的人，旅人便要求政府保護他們。

美國政府官員知道他們得做點事情，他們不希望礦工在那條路上受到攻擊，因此政府單位與紅雲和其他酋長開會，希望能找到解決辦法。開會時，紅雲看到軍隊在那條路上搭建堡壘，他發現這個會議一點意義也沒有，因為政府還是計畫讓這條路線保持暢通。紅雲氣壞了！

拉科塔族所有的部落團結一起，對堡壘展開攻擊，並殺死許多士兵。政府發現這條路太難守護，於是撤退了軍隊，拉科塔人便燒毀了堡壘。對於紅雲與他的族人來說，這是場重要的勝利。

紅雲戰役之後，他們在拉勒米堡簽訂條約。政府關閉了博茲曼小道，將達科他區大塊的土地撥給了拉科塔人，這區域包括了神聖的黑丘（Black Hills），拉科塔人相信黑丘就是他們部落的發源地。

1874 年，黑丘挖掘出金礦。來自國內各地的礦工侵犯了拉科塔人的聖地，讓拉科塔人感到非常難過，他們攻擊那些進入黑丘的人。政府想要買下黑丘，但是拉科塔人拒絕出售。

拉科塔酋長坐牛（Sitting Bull）和他的族人移居到小巨角河畔的夏日營地去，那裡也是夏安族搭營的地方。美國軍隊派遣部隊，強迫他們搬回保留區。

喬治·卡斯特將軍因為參與幾年南北戰爭而出名。他率領軍隊辛苦地前進，攻擊拉科塔族人。但印地安人的數量遠超過卡斯特的預期。最後，卡斯特將軍和他的部隊不但輸了那場戰役，也因此喪命。

Lesson 15 　哪些人是廢奴主義者？ P. 60

美國於 1787 年制定憲法時，國家的領導者們爭辯有關奴隸制度的議題，南方的領導者說服其他人維持奴隸制度的合法化。但過沒多久，教會的領袖們開始質疑奴隸制度是否正確。第一個站出來反對奴隸制度的團體是貴格會，他們想要終止全美國的奴隸制度。

到了 1800 年代早期，生活開始有了變化。美國北方與中部的人們不再使用奴隸，但是南方的幾個州拒絕廢除奴隸制度。許多人認為應該要強迫南方終止奴隸制度，這些人被稱為廢奴主義者，他們認為應該要讓所有的奴隸自由。

廢奴主義者知道他們在南方會面臨一場硬仗，因為南方人並不想廢除奴隸制度。大部分的人相信奴隸制度中最糟糕的部分就是奴隸交易與拍賣，廢奴主義者決定先解決這個部分。在爭辯許久之後，終於決定美國境內所有的奴隸交易必須在 1807 年前停止。

地下鐵道

有些奴隸企圖逃離主人，但大部分都會被捉回去，並受到處罰，有些甚至因此而喪命。廢奴主義者開始幫助他們之後，逃跑變得稍微容易一些。他們規劃了一條從南方逃到北方的幾個州和加拿大的路線，這條路線稱為「地下鐵道」。

地下鐵道並不像一般的鐵路有火車軌道，它被稱為「鐵道」是因為在通往自由的途中有許多停靠站；被稱為「地下」，是因為這是個秘密。在地下鐵道帶領大家通往自由的是車掌，而在這鐵道上旅行的奴隸則是乘客。

如果有奴隸想要逃跑，在南方的廢奴主義者會與他聯繫，這個人會告訴奴隸通往北方的第一個停靠站在哪裡，沿途中每個停靠站都會有人告訴那個逃跑的奴隸下一站在哪裡。有時候奴隸得藏匿在樹上、沼澤或穀倉裡，通常還會有奴隸追捕者在追捕這些奴隸。

有些廢奴主義者提供資訊，有些廢奴主義者會將奴隸藏在自己的家中，提供食物與衣物給他們，有些則擔任車掌的角色，這些人都是冒著自己的生命危險在幫助其他人獲得自由。

Lesson 16 建築用到的形狀 P. 64

韋德家想要在一塊土地上蓋棟新房子。這附近很適合韋德一家居住，因為他的爸媽就在附近上班，而他的朋友也住在這個區域。

韋德很想知道他們的新房子會是什麼樣子。他開始看各種的房屋，發現房子的設計有好幾種不一樣的形狀。

仔細的研究你家附近的房子或公寓，你會發現房子有許多種形狀。研究形狀的學問就叫做幾何學，而幾何學處處可見。

建築師設計房屋。韋德一家人和一位建築師會面，討論他們房子的樣子。建築師給他們看他最喜歡的建築物照片，一間消防局。

建築師挑選可以構成房屋以及房間的各種形狀。想想你自己的房子或公寓，它是由許多三度空間的形體所組成，長方形角柱與立方體都是很適合房間的 3D 形狀。

韋德家請來的建築師說明房間該怎麼放置，用來睡覺的臥室應該遠離像是廚房這類的吵雜空間。建築師讓韋德一家人看了幾張很棒的房屋照片，韋德和家人仔細的看著照片，看看是否可以從中得到一些靈感。韋德發現房子裡木樑和磚製的柱子看起來像是長方形角柱，屋子的每一面屋頂看起來都像是平面的長方形，他也看了一間小有名氣名叫「落水山莊」的房屋資料。

在家人們分享了他們所有的想法之後，建築師畫了個草稿，告訴他們房子蓋好之後的模樣。

Lesson 17 頭髮亂糟糟的一天 P. 68

當我被鬧鐘的尖銳聲吵醒時，我知道瑪莉莎已經氣急敗壞的扣好扣子。我的鬧鐘聲響不是排行榜上前 40 名的曲子，而是像貨物列車駛過隧道般大聲的喊喊呃呃靜電聲。我把摀住耳朵的枕頭拿開，把耳朵扭回原位之後，像隻蝸牛般拖著步伐走到走廊，等著輪我用浴室，好準備上學。

我那邪惡的妹妹像門階上的報紙一樣地靠在牆上，臉上掛著惡作劇般的笑容。她脫口而出：「妳的頭髮！看起來好像有烏鴉在妳頭上築巢一樣！」

我衝過去，手張的像禿鷹一般，把她的頭壓在地上。老爸立刻從浴室出來，臉上塗滿了刮鬍膏。當他大叫「放開妳妹妹！」時，一大滴的刮鬍膏滑進他嘴裡。那個味道嚐起來一定很糟，因為老爸的臉馬上就成了一隻變色龍，面色蒼白，然後出現綠色、黃色和粉紅色。

然後老爸看著我說：「可以整理一下妳那頭亂髮嗎？妳的頭髮看起來像是一團亂糟糟的刺！」

我看著走廊上的鏡子，鏡子裡的人盯著我瞧，默默的揶揄說：「很讚的頭髮！嘿嘿，他們可能會因為妳的頭髮，把妳關在動物園的籠子裡！」我抓起梳子，但是那玩意兒一靠近我不受控制的鬃毛時，就好像嚇得發抖求饒。我只好舉起白旗，尋求協助。

我感到十分沮喪，於是我走進媽媽的房間，求她幫幫我。她轉過來看著我，雙眼閃閃發光，但是她的聲音卻充滿了同情：「又是個頭髮亂糟糟的一天？」

「是啊！」我說。我坐在她的床邊，就好像在等醫生打針一樣。

她走過來，拖鞋默默無聲的在睡袍下移動著。她手上握著一把梳子，那尖利的牙齒閃閃發光，彷彿在說：「打結愈多愈好！」我的頭髮像是船上扭在一起的繩子，媽媽幫我梳頭髮時，我每分每秒都在害怕，我覺得至少有一億根頭髮從頭皮上被用力扯掉，我覺得我就要禿頭了。

但是最後我看向鏡子，我竟然變身了！在皇后小小的協助下，我是個打敗惡龍的公主！

Lesson 18 生物群落 P.72

不同種類的植物與動物生活在不一樣的生物群落。每個群落都有不同的環境：冷或熱，濕或乾。每個生物群落的狀態決定了哪些植物和動物可以居住在那裡。

苔原和針葉林帶

在地球極北的苔原生物群落區，天氣非常的寒冷，又強又冷的風吹過平坦的苔原。冬天時，最上層的土壤會結冰，夏天的時候融化。在它之下則是永遠結凍的一層，叫做永凍層。永凍層讓水流不出去，累積成池塘和沼澤。樹木無法在苔原區生長，因為它們的根無法穿透永久凍土層，因此，在苔原區生長的植物是草、苔蘚和地衣。苔原地區的動物則包括了北美馴鹿、狼、北極熊和雪地貓頭鷹。

在苔原區南邊的是地球上最大的陸上生物群落—針葉林帶，涵蓋了大部分的加拿大、蘇俄和中國。這裡的冬天又長又寒冷，而夏天則是又短又涼爽。針葉林帶擁有常綠的樹木，葉子在冬天也不會掉光。需要樹木的動物可以住在針葉林帶中，鳥可以在樹上築巢，而鹿則躲在陰暗處。

森林、草原和沙漠

在溫帶森林的南方，溫暖的氣候讓四季分明，而不是只有兩種氣候。有些溫帶森林的樹和灌木是落葉性的，表示它們的樹葉每年都會掉一次，常見的樹種如楓樹、毛山櫸和橡樹。春天和夏天的時候，樹葉會利用光合作用蒐集陽光，每棵植物都儲存了過冬所需要的能量，不需要樹葉的時候就讓它們掉光。鹿、浣熊、狐狸、兔子和松鼠等動物會在森林裡建造牠們的窩。

在夏天乾熱、冬天溫濕的地區會有草原生物群落。除了南極洲外，每塊大陸都有草原。在非洲，斑馬與長頸鹿在草原上吃草，而水牛曾經住在北美平原的草原上。草原上有高度不超過 10 呎高的常青灌木。

乾燥沙漠的生物群落很少有雨水，因為山擋住了帶來雨雲的風。白天時，陽光烤焦了土地，即使在陰暗處，溫度也能高達攝氏 50 度（華式 121 度）！但是到了夜晚，溫度會掉到接近 0 度。沙漠的植物適應了這種艱困的環境，有些具備了長長的覓水根，有些像仙人掌這類的植物，則將水分儲存在枝幹和根部。

Lesson 19 馬可‧范‧羅斯瑪倫：為生物多樣性而戰的鬥士 P.76

1997 年，有個來自亞馬遜盆地的印地安人來到了生物學家馬可‧范‧羅斯瑪倫在巴西的家。印地安人手裡拿著一個裝了一隻小猴子的錫罐，荷蘭人用手指戳了小毛球一下。小猴子害怕的吱吱叫。

范‧羅斯瑪倫差點驚喜的大叫出來，他是猩猩和猿猴的專家，但是他發現自己正盯著一種不知名的侏儒狨猴類物種，這是個驚人的發現。印地安人只知道在馬德拉河附近有人誘捕這種狨猴，而這條河流入亞馬遜盆地，這個線索讓范‧羅斯瑪倫展開了長達九個月的漫長探索之旅。

啟程

范‧羅斯瑪倫的探索帶領他進入亞馬遜一個從未被研究過的地區，這個地區生物多樣性豐富，到目前為止，他的團隊已經發現七種靈長類動物。他們還發現巴西堅果樹失蹤的近親，以及一種樹葉比大象耳朵還大的植物。最棒的是，范‧羅斯瑪倫發現一種古老耕種技術的遺跡，這個技術是由一萬多年前石器時代的部落所發明。

范‧羅斯瑪倫也研究藥用植物和雨林保留區。在南美洲，他研究樹窩裡的蜘蛛猴，常常以牠們咬過丟在地上的水果來裹腹。「我還滿餓的。」他回想著，「因為蜘蛛猴是非常節儉的食客。」

蜘蛛人

范‧羅斯瑪倫在雨林裡靜悄悄地穿過樹叢間，突然，雨滴從樹上落下，范‧羅斯瑪倫把他的雙筒望遠鏡往上一看，有樹枝彈了一下，跳出一隻他和團隊最近才辨識出的新品種猴類。

身為新有物種的發現者，范‧羅斯瑪倫有權為牠們命名，但是名聲對他來說一點也不重要，重要的是拯救了一塊亞馬遜純淨的綠色地區。他警告說：「如果不這麼做，在我們發現新的植物和動物之前，雨林就會被摧毀了。」

什麼是生物多樣性？

多樣化是生命的調味料，多樣化指的就是生物的多樣性。專家說地球上可能有約 300 萬到 3000 萬的物種。有些科學家相信到 2050 年，一半以上的物種將會絕種，很快地棲息地和周遭的環境會喪失它們的生物多樣性，舉例來說，當棲息地中某種植物消失時，以那種植物維生的動物也會隨之滅亡。

Lesson 20 迅猛龍 P. 80

迅猛龍是種小型的肉食性恐龍，牠活在 7500 萬年前左右，身型大約有七呎長，重量約 35 磅。從字面上來看，迅猛龍指的是「動作迅速的小偷」。化石證據顯示，這種小型恐龍一定是動作快速又有效率的獵食者。

牠的前腳像鳥爪一樣非常地瘦小，牠有長長的指頭和銳利的爪子，適合抓住獵物，又長又瘦的腿讓迅猛龍可以快速的捕捉獵物，牠的每隻腳都有巨大的爪子，可以在受害者身上留下很深的傷口。牠腳上的「致命爪子」非常的巨大，大到牠必須要把前腳舉起來，這樣牠才有辦法走路和奔跑。科學家認為迅猛龍可能是以群體的方式獵食，像現代的狼群一樣，以合作的方式來擊倒大型獵物。

迅猛龍有長長的頭和又小又尖的牙齒，牠的眼睛微微的向中間靠攏，這讓牠可以更準確地測量獵物的距離。

迅猛龍有條又長又細的尾巴，牠的尾巴因為有像骨頭般的筋絡而變得很強壯，讓牠在奔跑時可以保持平衡，當牠全速奔跑捕捉獵物時，尾巴也能幫助牠快速改變方向。

最近在蒙古發現迅猛龍的化石，這些化石顯示迅猛龍有羽毛。羽毛有助於保溫，也有助於吸引其他迅猛龍，或對其他迅猛龍發出信號。

「猛禽類」的恐龍有許多像鳥一樣可以適應環境的條件。也因為這樣，許多古生物學家相信現代的鳥類是由迅猛龍和牠的近親演化而來。

Lesson 21 一捆柴 P. 84

以前有個商人，他是位以三個優秀兒子為榮的驕傲父親。但是這幾個孩子總是吵個不停。商人常告訴他們，如果他們能共同合作，日子會更好過，但他們完全不理會他的忠告。

他們不斷的爭吵讓商人再也忍受不了，於是他想了一個辦法，要讓他們知道必須團結。他把所有的兒子都叫來，告訴他們說：「我的兒子啊，我無法再陪伴你們的日子就快來臨了。你們必須一起經營家族事業，學習信任彼此。但是依你們三個吵架的樣子來看，我無法想像你們能夠一起做出一番成就來。所以幫我做件事吧，去撿一捆柴來，將它用繩子綁好，帶來這裡。」

這些孩子帶著木柴回來後，父親又說了：「就這樣拿著那捆柴，把它折成兩半。你們哪一個人可以做到，就可以繼承我所有的財產。」

最大的兒子先試了試。他把膝蓋放在那捆柴上，用盡力氣地又壓又拉，但就是無法將那捆柴折彎。接著老二試了，最小的兒子也試了，卻沒有一個人成功，沒有人能將木柴折斷。

「爸爸，您給了我們一個不可能的任務。」他們嚷嚷著。商人點點頭，伸手拿了那捆柴，解開繩子，遞給每個兒子一人一根木柴。

「現在試試」他說。這三個兒子都輕易地用膝蓋把木柴折斷了。

商人接著問：「現在你們知道我的意思了嗎？你們一起合作，就會很強大，而你們的事業也會跟著成功。但是如果你們一直爭吵，每個人都用自己的方式，那你們的對手就會擊垮你們。」

Lesson 22 新爺爺 P.88

我們從旅行車下來，合成塑膠的印子印在我們腿的背面，終於到了奶奶離遊樂園只有幾分鐘遠的新家。

「我們是來這裡見你們的新爺爺。」爸媽提醒我們，而我和哥哥們發現排列在車道旁的樹上有柳丁，前門旁大籃子裡有檸檬和萊姆，還有像壘球一樣懸掛在樹枝上的葡萄柚。

奶奶和新爺爺在前門迎接我們。在等待和新爺爺抱抱和親吻時，我稍微觀望了一下他。新爺爺看起來不太新，老老的，就是一般爺爺的樣子。他抱我的時候，弄亂了我的頭髮，他的手臂很壯，而且不肯放開我，他小小聲地跟我說：「我猜妳一定等不及要去坐雲霄飛車了吧！」他竟然知道我們開了快三天車真正的理由耶！

我笑了。新爺爺唯一讓我覺得新的東西就只有房子吧，我不知道我們要睡在哪，也不會欣賞吊在餐廳桌上方的豪華枝形吊燈。我從來沒看過在玻璃後面閃閃發光的獎章，也沒看過駱駝鞍，或藏在蕨類植物中的象牙雕像。我不熟那條可以通往私人後院沙灘的紅磚小徑，也不了解那艘停靠在湖中的船。

但經過幾次造訪後，我對這房子愈來愈熟悉了。現在我有很多和新爺爺共渡的回憶。我們會一起待在湖上，我學滑水的時候，他會拉著我的滑水板。之後，他會坐在窗邊，看著我繞湖畔迴旋。我記得他會一次又一次地說我們最喜歡的故事─有關安那波里斯、戰爭和紫心勳章。

我的新爺爺對我來說，一點都不「新」。但是他給了我許多新回憶，而我也會永遠珍惜這些回憶─他的湖畔小屋、檸檬樹，當然，還有雲霄飛車。最重要的是，我記得爺爺的愛和他的慷慨大方。因為很久很久以前，我對他來說也是新的，而他對待我這個新孫女卻好像我們一直都在一起一樣。

Lesson 23 研究名字 P.92

「有什麼關係呢？玫瑰不叫玫瑰，依然芳香如故」──《羅密歐與茱麗葉》第二場第二幕

45698 田納西州芬芳市甜豆路 987 號

弗莉塔花店

45682 田納西州鬱金香市玫瑰巷 564 號

2008 年 9 月 15 日

親愛的女士：

在經過許多研究後，我已經找到您的名字和它的意義了。您的名字恰如其分地就是「平和」的意思。我說恰如其分，是因為好幾次我到您的店裡，發現您是那樣文靜隨興的人，在您四周的人都能感受到您沉穩的性格。您的聲音和獨特的格調不僅反映了個人內在的祥和，也讓周遭的人在這樣一個步調快速的世界裡，愉悅地感受到安全與從容。

研究您的名字是件愉快的事，對於這項服務，我完全不打算收費，因為我已經從認識那麼多良善的人，以及和他們魚雁往來中，得到應有的報酬。好好地享受您的名字和它所帶來的意涵吧。

艾薇娜·佛洛依德　敬上

Lesson 24 羨慕作家 P.96

我真的很敬佩作家。他們有善於表達的天賦，能夠透過文字影響人們，還有移情的才能。因為寫作是那麼地好玩，所以我很羨慕作家的工作。把自己的感受寫在紙上，對有些人來說很困難不是每個人都能用書寫文字來打開心房，與全世界分享交流；但對於有些人來說寫作是很容易的一件事，我覺得他們非常幸運。

作家在紙上創作故事，他們了解並尊重文字的力量。作家知道文字可以操弄、說服他人、使人動怒，或安撫人心，還可以引人發笑、哭泣，或是帶領人們到另一個世界。

作家是一群特別的人，他們願意冒險和其他人分享一部分自己的。他們寫進我心坎底，鼓勵我、慰藉我，有時候他們也鞭斥我，或是扮演我的良心。作家們一定也因為他們所書寫的文字會永遠

流傳下去而感到開心，這也是我很羨慕的一點。他們是一群很特別的人，能觸及我的內心，感動我的靈魂。有時候，我也會因為他們的一個小故事或是一句引言久久無法自己。

Lesson 25 上下顛倒 P. 100

你眼睛看到的東西其實是上下顛倒的。光線進入瞳孔後，抵達位於虹膜後方的晶體，晶體具有將光線聚焦在眼球後部的重要任務。而眼球的後部為視網膜，視網膜的作用就像電影螢幕一樣，但是在你眼球中的電影卻是上下顛倒的。光線透過晶體到達視網膜後，視網膜會傳送訊息到大腦，而大腦接收到的訊息也是上下顛倒的。但是我們的大腦很聰明，它會把接受到的圖像倒過來，所以圖像就變正了。

你知道你的眼睛看到的東西是上下顛倒的嗎？真的！我們眼睛接收到的影像其實上下顛倒，是大腦把它翻轉過來，所以你看到的影像才是正的。很令人驚訝吧！

Lesson 26 阿茲特克城 P. 104

數百年前，阿茲特克人一族決定找個新家。他們不知道該去哪找，但是他們的太陽神允諾他們土地。祂說，叼著一條蛇的老鷹所停歇的仙人掌那裡，就是他們的住所。而阿茲提克人在墨西哥中部找到了這個地方。

阿茲特克人將他們的新城市命名為特諾奇提特蘭，它位在湖中央的一座小島上，是個極佳的地點。他們在沼澤地開墾浮動的菜園進行耕種，這些園地是將樹枝聚集在一起，然後在上面填土而成，作物的根經常穿過土壤進到水底。玉米、豆子、紅番椒和蕃茄都是阿茲特克常見的作物。

阿茲特克人修築運河，利用獨木舟在城裡往來。除此之外，他們也建造了橫跨湖泊連接主要大陸的公路。如果他們受到戰爭的威脅，就把公路移除，這樣一來，除非敵人有船，不然他們是抵達不了島上的。短短幾年，阿茲特克人建造了宮殿、廟宇、球場，甚至還有一座動物園。

阿茲特克成了當時最著名的帝國之一，他們是老練的戰士，知道如何在戰役中獲勝，1519 年西班牙探險隊抵達前，他們幾乎是無敵的。一開始，

阿茲特克人相信西班牙人是神，但是帶著槍枝和受過精良訓練的西班牙人卻擊敗了阿茲特克人，接收了他們的城市。

Lesson 27 第二章：病毒——我們周遭的病菌 P. 108

主題

我們活在一個充滿微生物的世界裡，微生物是用顯微鏡才看得到的生物，像是病毒、細菌、真菌。一湯匙的泥土裡包含了數十億的微生物，從你的頭到腳，由裡到外，全身都是無數微生物的收容所。大多數的微生物是無害的，而且很多其實是好的，可以幫我們消化食物。但有些也會讓我們生病，我們稱那些不好的為細菌或病菌。

偷襲

細菌會透過鼻子、嘴巴或其他的孔隙進入我們體內，它們也可能經由皮膚上的傷口進入。但如果細菌真的無所不在，那為什麼我們不會一直生病呢？

大多數的時候，我們的身體會擊退細菌。但如果沒有充足的睡眠或飲食不均衡，你的抵抗力，也就是擊退疾病的能力就會下降，那麼細菌就很容易進行偷襲。

細菌如何散播

只要一個噴嚏就可以讓上百萬細菌進入空氣中，遮掩咳嗽的手也會將細菌留在書桌、門把和電腦鍵盤上。此外，疾病還會以其他各種方式散播，我們也會因為烹調或處理不當的食物上的細菌而生病，水也可能被原蟲等細菌感染，特別是在貧窮國家。

目標：小孩

孩童，特別是幼兒，比成人更容易生病。其中一個原因是他們的身體還沒有掌握辨認及對抗常見細菌的技巧。免疫系統的細胞負責對抗細菌，隨著我們年紀增長，這些「士兵」會越來越擅長抵抗傳染病。這樣一來，就可以對抗那些會讓孩童時期的我們生病的細菌了。

Lesson 28　古代中國　P. 112

第一批中國人在黃河河谷定居下來，他們都是農夫和工匠，除了種植穀物之外，他們也製作陶器和產絲。第一個群聚社會是夏朝。所謂朝代，就是由一個家族掌管某個國家的權力超過一段時間，夏朝約從西元前 2000 年掌權到西元前 1600 年。中國邊境的山脈將夏朝與其他國家隔開來，所以在那段時間，並沒有太多的通商往來。

商朝

商朝掌權的時間大約是西元前 1600 年到西元前 1046 年，當時人們利用青銅來製作工具和車輪。最早的中國書寫系統就從那個時候開始，人們將文字刻在動物的殼跟骨頭上，稱為甲骨文。

長壽的周朝

接下來的周朝延續了九百年，這個朝代以書寫的方式，把發生的事情記錄下來。周朝末代帝王非常地積弱不振，無法管理人民，很多小城邦脫離統治，彼此爭戰。很快地，內戰就爆發了，上千人死於血腥的戰事中，農村都被毀了。

短暫但美好的秦朝

接著秦朝取代了衰敗的周朝。秦朝只維持了 15 年，但秦始皇在短暫的時間內造就許多事蹟。他結束了接連不斷的戰爭，統一了整個國家，掌管整個中國。

前幾年，其他的領導者修築城牆來保衛自己的領土。秦始皇決定把這些城牆連接起來，讓它們變得更長，這就是中國萬里長城的起源。

漢朝

秦始皇過世後，他的兒子無力統治整個國家，於是漢朝就興起了。漢朝持續了四百多年，是中國歷史上最強盛的朝代之一。這段期間，中國的人口達到六千萬人，使中國成為世界上最大的國家。從中國到歐洲的通商之路─絲路，也是在這時候完成。它是第一條連接亞洲與歐洲國家的道路。

漢朝一滅亡，戰爭時期隨之到來。異族統治了中國北部，而中國南部則由不同的統治者各據一方。

Lesson 29　如果學校餐廳裡的原子會說話　P. 116

經過餐廳牆壁時，我聽到了一陣低語，所以我把耳朵靠近牆壁一點。我覺得一定是我在幻想，但是似乎又很真實，牆上的一個原子正輕聲地說著它過去幾年來所知道的秘密。這對我來說，可真是個千載難逢的機會啊！美國總統 40 年前也唸過這所學校，或許我可以發現關於我們國家領導人的一些趣事。

什麼！我的體育老師曾在這所學校跟總統當同學？老師也亂丟過食物，還惹過麻煩，他還真是個狠角色啊！牆上的原子全都看到，也聽說了。這真可以說是有趣的一天啊！

午餐時間只有 20 分鐘，但是我想要充分地利用這每分每秒。我拉了張椅子坐下來，專心地聽在這間餐廳裡所發生的事。我悄聲地提問，然後聆聽回覆。我得到學校、行政部門、教職員和總統的消息，我等不及要把一些八卦傳出去了。

突然間，我的體育老師把手搭在我肩上，他彎下身，小聲地恭喜我發現這面也提供他情報的牆，並警告我不能談論這面會說話的牆。他答應我，他不會告訴任何人我認為牆壁會說話的事，只要我不把聽到的秘密說出去。

午餐時間結束了，我衝出餐廳往教室去。我無意間聽到體育老師悄悄地跟我說：「別忘了我們的約定─會說話的牆。」但不知怎麼地，我知道他是從個人經驗的角度告誡我。不過我很確定的是，我會永遠嚴守這些秘密，不讓任何人知道。

Lesson 30　考試　P. 120

蘿拉打了個呵欠，還把手臂伸直高過她的頭。她的脊椎發出三聲刺耳的喀拉喀拉聲，在安靜的教室裡回蕩著，幾個學生咯咯地笑著。小島老師瞪了一眼整間教室，然後把考卷放在凱莉桌上。凱莉吸了一口氣，迅速地翻了一下考卷，一共有五張。全班振筆疾書時，小島老師就在走道上來回走動。他破舊的平跟船鞋規律的扣扣作響，和時鐘一塊兒提醒我們時間。凱莉瞄了一眼門上的時鐘，還有三十分鐘。

凱莉緊張地拉了自己的長辮子，把頭左右伸展了一下。一開始她閉著雙眼，後來她張開眼睛時看到蘿拉彎起的左手裡有一張紙條！當小島老師的扣扣聲接近時，她的左手偷偷地藏到桌子底下，等老師走後，再拿上來看答案。

凱莉把她的椅子拉近書桌，刺耳的聲音讓她起雞皮疙瘩，也讓其他人打了寒顫。她每一題都有寫上答案，憶起和媽媽一起唸書、小島老師的課後輔導、反覆閱讀的筆記和背誦的內容，而非去購物中心、棒球賽或看電影。

凱莉有幾題的答案很確定，而有些她只能盡力作答。

蘿拉最先寫完。同學們看著她走到前面，把考卷放在小島老師的桌上，連小島老師看起來都很驚訝。

蘿拉回到座位後，悠閒地用擦著粉紅色指甲油的手梳著及肩的金髮，然後輕敲桌面。

代表下課的鈴聲聽起來很像指揮朝樂隊示意開始演奏的口哨聲，凱莉把她的考卷放在小島老師手中的一堆考卷上。她寫完了，但沒有時間檢查。

她和幾個同學眼神相會。感覺到一種考試終於結束的放鬆，和「是啊，它真的結束了」的悲傷混合而成的複雜情緒。

凱莉不知道自己是否還能面對蘿拉，但她們共用一個置物櫃，還擁有一些共同的回憶。她可以接受和一個作弊的人當朋友嗎？

Review Test

漫長的西進之路 P. 124

摘要：許多美國人移民到西部開始新生活。
背景：到了 1820 年，美國領土和各州上的人口已經成倍數成長。人們開始冀望到西部生活。拜新建的運河、道路和鐵路所賜，到西部已經比以往容易多了。但還是有個難以到達的地區，那就是：奧勒岡區。這個廣大的地區是由現今的奧勒岡州、華盛頓州、愛達荷州和英屬哥倫比亞組成。

開路先鋒

到奧勒岡區最容易的方式卻也是最慢的：搭船繞整個南美洲，這可能得花上一年的時間。而最直接的方式就是走陸路穿過北美大平原：包括奧克拉荷馬州、堪薩斯州、內布拉斯加州、達科他州、蒙大拿州，以及部分的懷俄明州與科羅拉多州。

了解北美大平原這地區的唯一美國人就是山地人（mountain men），也就是那些以土地維生的皮草交易商。其中有一位山地人傑帝達・史密斯，帶領第一批探險隊到奧勒岡區。1832 年，他帶領納薩恩・惠氏和其他 24 人從密蘇里州的聖路易斯出發到西部去。史密斯帶著這群人，穿過了洛磯山脈中被稱為南方隘口的峽谷進入奧勒岡。

1834 那年，惠氏的奧勒岡之行改變了歷史，探險隊員將奧勒岡美景傳回東部，人們聽聞了奧勒岡蘊藏無盡的樹木、水和魚類等大自然美景的故事，而創造出了一股「奧勒岡熱潮」。

奧勒岡古道

通往奧勒岡的路徑被稱為奧勒岡古道。從 1843 年到 1868 年，大約有五十萬人從這條路到奧勒岡以及猶他州和加州，大部分的男人、女人和孩子們搭乘大篷車從密蘇里出發，有時候整支隊伍由牛或騾子所拉的上百輛大篷車組成。這些旅程都非常地艱辛，有些拓荒者在危險的溪流、河川中溺斃，或失去了所有的家當；有些因為閃電、馬車意外，或耗盡飲水和食物而喪命。有時候（並不是常常）懷有敵意的印第安人也會構成威脅。途中最可怕的災難就是霍亂，那是一種透過糟糕的衛生條件所散佈的致命惡疾。

約翰・傅里蒙

約翰・傅里蒙是一位在 1842 年和 1843 年踏上奧勒岡古道的探險家。他想鼓勵在東部的人們移居到西部。於是他寫了許多報導，描述那段旅程有多麼簡單。這些報導的確激勵了人們前往西部，但其實大多數的文章並不是約翰・傅里蒙所撰，而是由他的妻子潔西・貝登執筆。

食物

奧勒岡古道的拓荒者必須確定自己為這趟旅程準備了足夠的食物。一位開拓者寫道，他需要至少200 磅的麵粉、150 磅的培根、十磅的咖啡、20磅的糖，和 10 磅的鹽。為了一趟兩千英里的旅程，一家四口需要大約一千磅的食物。

傑夫日誌 P.126

8月23日

我整個腦袋想的都是紅藍大戰，那是卡卡諾穆夏令營中最大的活動。在每年夏天將近尾聲時，整個營隊就會分成兩隊：紅隊和藍隊，最後得分最多的那一隊就能得到獎品。我們紅隊最棒了！

第一場比賽就在今天下午。我不喜歡輔導員把我和泰分開。如果我能跟我最好的朋友同一隊，那就太棒了。不過我想就算我們現在是敵人，還是可以維持好哥兒們的關係。但是問題是，每個人都只和自己的隊友混在一起，如果你和藍隊的人說話，就好像你是個叛徒一樣。

今天下午是游泳比賽，我游的是接力賽的部分。輪到我的時候，我們原本是落後的，但是我追上了泰，而且還超過他。最後紅隊贏了，每個人都來跟我擊掌。我瞄了泰一眼，他看起來真的很生氣，我們握了手，卻沒說什麼話。

輔導員叫我們要展現運動家的精神，但是他們也一直叫我們要贏過對方。在睡舖上，我們大喊：「紅隊最棒！」他們也大聲地回說：「藍隊加油！」在不同隊的人，都不再對彼此表示友好了，這有點詭異。在睡舖上我問泰：「你過的還好嗎？」他只是聳聳肩。

但不管怎樣，紅隊就是得贏。

8月24日

上午我們比籃球。亞麗珊卓真的很棒，她投進了15分，我則拿了12個籃板，而且我們擊敗了藍隊，以45比37獲勝。午餐後，我在電腦室玩遊戲。藍隊的一些人包括泰，從我背後看我玩電腦，試圖要惹火我。只要我輸的時候，他們就會歡呼。我告訴泰，他可以選個電腦遊戲，我一定會盡我所能打敗他，但他只是嘲笑我，然後就和他的隊友走開了。我氣炸了。

下午：乒乓球比賽（不是我的強項，所以我沒參加）。排球，我們輸了。還有射箭，但我不是俠盜羅賓漢，所以泰狠恨地擊敗了我。我很生氣，因為我讓全隊失望了。我覺得我聽到泰在批評我，所以他過來要跟我擊掌的時候，我完全不理他。不過後來我覺得我這樣有點糟糕，但是我的隊友說我這樣做很酷。誰還需要泰啊？

8月25日

紅藍大戰的最後一天是田徑賽。兩隊的比數很接近。在短跑和接力賽後，我們落後藍隊五分，所以不管哪一隊能在長跑中獲勝，他們就能贏得紅藍大戰。

這長跑賽是很嚴酷的。我們跑上主要道路後，繞湖一周，然後再沿著有做標記的道路進到樹林裡。我被樹枝打到，還被石頭絆倒了兩次。我回頭看，見到泰一路踩著軋軋聲前進。不一會兒，我的肺像著火般，我不得不停下來彎腰休息。當我這樣做時，泰超過我了。我盡可能地快跑，拉近和他的距離。我們兩個都衝刺到終點線，兩隊都像瘋了一樣地大叫著。但是泰以一碼或許是兩碼的距離贏過了我。紅隊因為我輸掉了紅藍大戰。

我覺得很丟臉，想躲起來。泰走過來跟我說：「很棒的比賽」，還伸出手來。因為每個人都在看我，所以我無力的握了一下他的手，然後我就走開了。

後來，我突然想通了一件事。我在美術跟工藝是做了很多東西，但是我在整個夏令營做的最棒的一件事就是交了一個朋友啊。誰會想要因為一些愚蠢的運動競賽就失去朋友呢？稍晚，我走向泰，向他恭喜。他把手搭在我的肩上，然後我們就一起到點心吧去了。我們又變回好哥兒們了！